He twirled a strand **P9-CQI-090**
his finger. "Weren't you the one who said scientists are curious?"

"They are."

He let her hair go, lowering his voice. "So aren't you curious about me?"

"I have a theory about you."

"Let's hear it."

She shook her head, aroused by his heated gaze. "No, I want to prove it or disprove it first."

"How?"

"Kiss me."

His gaze dropped to her body. "Do I get to choose where?"

She lifted his chin and tapped her mouth. "On the mouth," she said, although his sensuous look made her feel naked.

He feigned disappointment. "Just the mouth?"

"You can choose another spot later."

"Good."

When his lips touched hers, she discovered everything she had wanted to. His lips were both sweet and spicy, and they made her forget herself. Soon his kisses made a warm, wet path down her throat. "Have you proven your theory?" he asked, his breath warm against her skin.

"I'm still not sure."

Books by Dara Girard

Harlequin Kimani Romance

Sparks
The Glass Slipper Project
Taming Mariella
Power Play
A Gentleman's Offer
Body Chemistry
Round the Clock
Words of Seduction
Pages of Passion
Beneath the Covers
All I Want Is You
Secret Paradise
A Reluctant Hero
Perfect Match
Snowed in with the Doctor

Harlequin Kimani Arabesque

Table For Two
Gaining Interest
Carefree
Illusive Flame

DARA GIRARD

fell in love with storytelling at an early age. Her romance writing career happened by chance when she discovered the power of a happy ending. She is an award-winning author whose novels are known for their sense of humor, interesting plot twists and witty dialogue. When she's not writing, she enjoys spring mornings and autumn afternoons, French pastries, dancing to the latest hits and long drives.

Dara loves to hear from her readers. You can reach her at contact dara@daragirard.com or P.O Box 10345, Silver Spring, MD 20914.

SNOWED IN WITH THE *Doctor*

DARA GIRARD

HARLEQUIN® KIMANI™ ROMANCE

Recycling programs
for this product may
not exist in your area.

ISBN-13: 978-0-373-86334-1

SNOWED IN WITH THE DOCTOR

Copyright © 2013 by Sade Odubiyi

HARLEQUIN®

Printed in U.S.A.

www.Harlequin.com

Dear Reader,

"Mistletoe and Misunderstanding"—that's how the original idea for this story came to me. I wanted to write about three things that fascinate me: 1) the holidays, 2) how opposites attract and 3) sickle-cell research. At first, I wasn't sure I could pull it off, but I liked the challenge.

Fortunately, the right people fell into place: rash, hotheaded Dr. Lora Rice and cool, methodical Dr. Justin Silver. These two biomedical researchers put my story into action, with a passion for their work and each other. The holiday season helped add a touch of magic to their romance in a way that surprised even me.

I hope you enjoy this story about family, healing and, of course, true love.

All the best,

Dara Girard

Prologue

She couldn't believe it had finally arrived. Lora Rice ripped open the small brown package, then eagerly pulled out the item inside. She swept her hand over the raised letters on the cover of the book she'd ordered: *30 Days to Romance*. Just reading the title gave her shivers of anticipation. Late one night, a week ago, she'd been lazing on the couch in front of the TV with a half-eaten box of chocolate bonbons when a beautiful woman had appeared on the screen.

"Tired of sitting home alone on a Friday night? Do you sometimes wonder if Mr. Right will ever come? If you have, I've got the answer for you. Yes, he will. But you have to be ready for him."

"How?" Lora wondered aloud.

"How, you might ask? With my book 30 Days to Romance *you'll learn the skills necessary to attract the man of your dreams. Whether you're shy and plain or beautiful but awkward, I'll give you step-by-step guides and exercises to get you out of your shell and into the life of romance. If I can do it, so can you."*

That night Lora had sat up and listened to the testimonials, then ordered the book. Now it was here. Contrary to what her family thought, she was ready for roses and champagne. She wanted a date who remembered her name and didn't forget his wallet. She didn't want to spend another holiday avoiding the office party or family get-togethers. And lately it seemed like her family's only reason to exist was to set her up on a blind date or discuss what was wrong with her love life.

"You're nearly thirty-seven," her mother had said only a few weeks ago.

"I'm thirty-one."

"Oh, really? You look much older."

"Thanks, Mom."

"And if I think you're older, so will men, and they like their women young."

"Not always."

"The clock is ticking."

Lora didn't care about the clock. It was the pity she hated. She'd been a wallflower all her life. She didn't need to look in the mirror to know what everyone else saw. A slender woman of medium height with black square glasses and thick black hair always pulled back in a ponytail or bun. She didn't consider herself a stunning beauty and never turned heads. A man had never winked at her or even whistled. And she'd tried.

Lora remembered years ago that she had gone to her favorite department store and picked out a colorful pink spring dress, which she matched with a paisley lime-green short linen jacket. She had even bought a new pair of two-inch sling-back heels. After pulling her hair into a large braid, she had courageously walked past a construction site nearby, but she hadn't even gotten a glance.

At birthday parties, anniversaries and the occasional family gathering, she was overlooked and invisible. But she hadn't cared much while she was in school. All that had mattered to her then were her grades. Her classes got her out of the house and away from her father's critical stare. She'd flourished in high school, college and graduate school. How she looked or fit in was never a concern; she was in all honors classes, so she could hide behind her accomplishments. In high school she was president of the science club, and in college she excelled in her biology and chemistry classes, to the point that she was selected by two of her professors to work on several exciting grant-funded projects. Graduate school, where she had studied biomedical research, had been grueling, but Lora loved the challenge, and as always, she came out on top, winning several science awards. A white lab coat had been her primary outfit for the past eight years.

Then her best friend died. Suzette had been anything but invisible. She'd been a bright, vivacious Spanish blonde who made Lora's life feel like a big adventure. They'd gone to concerts together and learned tai chi. But when Suzette died, Lora's life of adventure seemed to go with her. She'd buried herself in her work as a researcher. One day when she was walking back to her office, she'd seen this sad, haggard woman in a store window, and it had taken her several moments to realize it was her own reflection. This was not the life Suzette would've wanted for her. She was the only person who'd really known Lora. Now, with the help of this book the old Lora would fade away and a new one would be born. Lora Rice would no longer be ignored, especially by one man: Warren Rappaport. He was a newly hired scientist in the department, and he was very sexy.

She'd achieved all that she wanted and was a success in her career. Now she was ready to be a success at love.

Chapter 1

November

Dr. Justin Silver was knockout gorgeous. It was a shame he was such a jerk. Why, of all the labs in the entire world, had he come to work in hers? It had been a cruel twist of fate to have to see—let alone work with—a man she'd never wanted to set eyes on again. Lora had joined Ventico Labs to work under Dr. Shirley Coolidge, a former professor she'd adored, and to research sickle cell anemia. Then Silver had been hired to replace the former director who'd overseen the three lab teams at Ventico. The other two teams were run by Dr. Kevin Yung, who focused on juvenile diabetes, and Dr. Carla Petton, who focused on effective pain management for the elderly. She'd cringed at the thought of working with Silver, but because she hardly saw him and only heard his name once in a while, she had discovered that his presence hadn't made much of a difference.

That was before the unthinkable happened. Dr. Coolidge left unexpectedly to take care of her sick mother, leaving a vacancy open that Silver had to fill until they hired a new manager. So for the past several months she'd had to deal with him, and now she found herself in his office for her performance evaluation.

When she'd first entered his office, for some reason the thought of desert sands and an ancient Mali palace came to her mind. He had the regal bearing of a king and acted as if he were lord and master of all.

Lora studied him as he sat behind an enormous glass-and-chrome desk, which was organized with military precision or obsessive compulsion, she didn't know which, nor did she care. He was a difficult man to categorize. His large office, which was enviable in their small facility, had several large windows with a view of the office complex with its manicured lawns and lake. But he didn't seem to take any pride in his status as director at Ventico Labs. His office was stark and about as welcoming as a broken-glass chair. No pictures were on display on the desk or on the walls; only a large erasable calendar and a Baltimore Ravens cap that sat on a chair in the corner stood out.

The one bit of whimsy was a small silver sculpture that sat on his desk. She couldn't make out what it was supposed to be, but it looked like macaroni and kidney beans sprayed with silver paint. Something a small child would make. It was positioned next to a large thermos that looked like it could hold enough food for a family of four. The second incongruous item in the room was the chair she sat in. It was sur-prisingly—almost annoyingly so—comfortable.

Lora hadn't expected that and wondered if the se-lection had been accidental. He wasn't the type to care about the comfort of others, just about getting the job done. He was a man of precision.

Lora flexed her fingers, pushing the sound of his voice to the background as he continued discussing her one-year evaluation. She found his voice unnerving. It was alarmingly deep and almost soothing and as decep-tive as an ocean's wild undercurrent. His voice could make a person ignore what he was actually saying. It could lull a person into agreeing with him, even when you didn't plan to. She could see why he was so suc-cessful as a director. No one argued with him. It was always "Yes, Dr. Silver." "Of course, Dr. Silver." But she wouldn't be conned. Lora knew who he really was. She listened closely to each word and let them cut right through her while she silently planned her revenge.

He'd said that her lab notes, usually handwritten, weren't always well organized or coherent enough. That, at times, she jumped to conclusions without stating adequate justification. But his most cutting assessment had been when he'd called her undisci-plined. Undisciplined? She was one of the best re-searchers in the lab, and she wasn't being modest.

She had always been the best. High school valedic-torian, youngest student to graduate from the Johns Hopkins School of Medicine Research doctoral pro-gram. Upon her arrival at Ventico Labs, she'd quickly organized several systems there that helped it run efficiently. And not only that, but people actually liked her. Unlike him. Nobody liked Justin Silver, not that they'd say so to his face. He wasn't someone to like. He was someone to follow, perhaps admire, even reluctantly respect because of his brilliance as a research scientist. But likable? Absolutely not.

She knew the moment she'd seen him again that it would be difficult, but she wouldn't think about their first meeting right now. He couldn't hold that against her, could he? They were adults—scientists—and they dealt with facts, not emotions. But with this evaluation Lora knew she wouldn't be granted the transfer she wanted to work on a project with Dr. Petton. Not only would the transfer allow her to work under a new head, but collaborating on Carla's project on the use of non-addictive pain medication would greatly advance her study of pain management and sickle cell anemia. Silver was halting her progress and stunting her career growth—and she couldn't fight him.

"Dr. Rice?"

Lora blinked then cleared her throat. "Yes?"

"Do you have any questions?"

Plenty. Such as whether he had a heart or if he rusted in the rain like the Tin Man. She brushed imaginary lint from her lap. "No."

"I'm surprised," he said coolly.

Lora took care to keep her gaze lowered, pushing up her glasses before they slid down her nose. Avoiding his gaze was her best defense. The best way to remain civil. "Why?"

"It's not like you to agree with everything I say."

That was true. But what was also true was that

he was trying to bait her. She knew she had to tread carefully. She needed to end the meeting and leave. "This is an evaluation. Whether I agree with your assessment is immaterial."

Dr. Silver leaned forward. It wasn't an aggressive move, but it put her on notice. "That doesn't stop me from being curious as to your feedback."

Lora nodded, straightening the cuff of her sleeve. No, she wouldn't tell him anything. She'd let him wonder. "Most scientists are curious. That's why we're in this field."

"You're so angry you can't even look at me."

Lora stiffened, sensing the challenge. Not just in his words, but also in his tone. That deep, slow timbre held a hint of mockery. But she wouldn't let him mock her. She was a different woman now. Different from the one he'd first met. She'd completed fourteen days of her *30 Days to Romance* project. Her progress had been slow, but she was determined to succeed. This was going to be a new season for her. She'd no longer be the wallflower.

She lifted her gaze. The moment she did, she knew she'd made a huge tactical error. Silver's voice was dangerous, but his eyes were lethal. They weren't just brown—they were like petrified wood, as if any emotion that had once been there had been frozen in time. Nothing was left but cold stone. At that moment she realized that Dr. Justin Silver was one of the most coldly calculating men she'd ever met. Just being in his presence gave her goose bumps.

Again, the desert sands image came to mind. He looked as if he came from a legion of warriors. She could picture him riding into battle, his brown skin polished by the sun, and conquering whoever he deemed his enemy. He had a warrior's arrogance and cunning. Aside from his steady brown eyes, he had a firm mouth that was solid like a blade and a ridged jawline. His eyelashes were the only problem. They were graceful and beautiful, and it annoyed her that they were wasted on such a man.

But she knew he was not a man to make either a friend or an enemy out of. Lora shifted in her seat. She was required to stay on his team and didn't want to do anything to jeopardize her position. She boldly held his cold gaze, determined to keep her composure. "I'm not upset," she said, pleased by the neutrality of her tone.

His voice grew soft and remained low. "Yes, you are."

Lora sighed, hoping to appear bored, although inside she was steaming. "May I leave now?"

"I'm not holding our first meeting against you, if that's what you're thinking."

"I wasn't thinking that," she said, wishing he hadn't brought it up. She hated that he remembered and mentioned it so casually, as if it didn't matter.

He frowned, confused. "Then why are you upset?"

"I didn't say I was upset."

"You don't need to. I can tell."

"I'm sure you can. You're very observant, after all. I just know you don't care." She stood, calculating her distance to the door. "Now excuse me."

"I do care."

Lora bit her lip to keep from laughing.

He raised his brows. "You don't believe me?"

"Does it matter?"

"Yes, I can't allow what happened in the past to affect our relationship now. I've moved past it, but obviously you haven't."

"I have. And I'm trying to be polite."

"Then stop and be honest."

"And risk losing my job?" she shot back, her patience thinning.

"You won't lose your job."

Lora returned to her seat and sat. "Is that a promise?"

Silver fell silent and leaned back, a casual gesture that was anything but. "I already know what you think of me, and I know you're not shy with voicing your opinion, so why start now? Although you are one of the best scientists we have here at Ventico, there's always room for improvement."

"I agree. May I go now?" Lora saw his eyes narrow, but she wouldn't give him the satisfaction of letting him know what she thought. She'd done that before, and it hadn't changed anything.

"Yes."

She stood again and walked to the door, feeling a small sense of victory.

"So what happened to your hair?"

Her hand flew to her hair as if she feared it had disappeared. She spun around and glared at him. "What do you mean?"

"It's different."

"I know." Lora gaped at him, trying to figure out if he was joking, but his tone wasn't mocking and his expression remained interested. Why was he casually talking about her hair? How had he noticed it? No one else seemed to. She'd gotten a trim and permed her thick hair to make it more manageable. She now wore it in a low, soft ponytail, using a decorative comb to hold it in place instead of a rubber band, and she'd added thin bangs and light brown highlights but nothing dramatic.

His eyes caught and held hers. "Whatever you did, it looks nice."

Lora blinked, unable to respond. Was that a compliment? Had she fallen into a parallel universe? She turned to the door, eager to escape. It didn't matter. He could be nice all he wanted, but that didn't change the fact she thought he was a bastard.

Lora left Silver's office, sat down at her desk and wanted to scream and kick something. Why did he criticize her one moment and compliment her the next? He was playing games. Yes, Justin Silver would get his payback.

"How did it go?" Carla asked. She was in her early forties, and Lora had met her briefly several years ago but had gotten to know her better while working at Ventico. She was slim with a face best suited for an operatic tragedy. Her lips turned down, and she had large somber brown eyes. She kept to herself. Lora knew she was single, never married, with an excellent mind. She was always very calm, as if she could walk through a storm without flinching. She'd helped Lora through the transition after Dr. Coolidge left and Dr. Silver took over. But although Carla was observant, she hadn't noticed Lora's new hairstyle—or at least she hadn't mentioned it. No one had, not even

Warren who she wanted to. Why had Silver noticed? Why had he said anything? "I'm still in one piece," Lora said with a nonchalance she didn't feel.

"Lucky you. He nearly made Dr. Yung cry with—"

"I don't care what he says to me. I know he can be mean." She'd never let herself care enough to let him hurt her. She was angry but not hurt.

"No, he—"

"How was your eval?"

"It was fine, but from your expression and tone I think I can surmise that we won't be working closely together."

"No. He effectively shot that possibility down." She clenched her hand into a fist and shook it at his closed door. "He's ruining my career."

Carla laughed. "It's not like you to be so dramatic. He's a savvy director and has a keen eye for what's best for us and our department."

"He moves us around like chess pieces."

"He's used to winning."

"So did he say anything specific?" Lora asked.

"Not really. I got good marks. I'm truly hoping he'll allow more funding for my project."

"You deserve it. I can't see him not letting that happen."

But as Lora said the words, she knew it was a lie. She could easily see him stopping Carla. Just as he had stopped her. If he didn't think something was worthwhile, he would disregard it. But she didn't care what he thought of her. He could think whatever he wanted. He was the type to always find fault anyway. But why had he given her a compliment? What was wrong with him? What was wrong with her? She wanted to stop thinking about him. Her make-over plan was supposed to *impress* men, but he didn't count.

In following the steps in *30 Days to Romance,* she'd already gotten a new pair of designer glasses. She'd tried contacts years ago but had never been able to adjust to them, and she had no interest in laser surgery. She'd also changed her hairstyle and even started wearing lipstick. She wasn't averse to wearing makeup; she just hadn't made it a priority. She'd even taken two dance lessons and was learning the salsa.

"I wonder what *his* evaluation was like," Carla said as she peered at an attractive black man hurrying past.

Lora looked up and saw Warren Rappaport walking by; she hoped she wasn't visibly drooling. She'd give *him* high marks all around. When Rappaport had arrived, most of the women had taken notice, but Carla hadn't shown much interest. She never seemed to take interest in men, or women, for that matter. Her main focus was her work, just as it had always been for Lora.

"Have you talked to him yet?" Carla asked, knowing of Lora's interest.

"Not yet."

"Personally, if I had to choose between Rappaport and Silver, I'd go for Silver."

"Are you insane?"

Carla held up her hands in surrender. "I know he's terrifying and a bit distant—"

"As far as the Arctic."

"But he's established, respected and easier to read.

Warren is attractive, I admit, but he's still building his career, and he's a little *too* charming."

"How can a man be too charming? Everyone likes him."

"Hmm. He just doesn't seem as transparent as he acts. I hope that book you're reading tells you how to catch the *right* man."

"How do you know about my book?" Lora asked, surprised.

"I saw it in your bag. You better be careful about reading it in here. And whose interest you get." She grinned, then walked away.

Lora folded her arms. Silver's response was an aberration, that was all. It had to be. She had holiday plans, and Dr. Justin Silver would not be part of them. But Dr. Warren Rappaport definitely would be.

Justin touched two fingers to the inside of his wrist, then checked his watch. He measured the time and his beating pulse, then swore. Yep, his pulse was racing. He could feel it but wanted to confirm it. This was the effect Lora Rice had on him. It had been the same the first time they'd met, when she'd basically let him know that she thought he was the scum of the earth. Unfortunately, it was no different now. No, he was wrong, it was worse. Much worse. And he wasn't sure what to do about it.

He found himself thinking of her skin, which was the color of roasted cocoa beans. Her lovely light brown eyes were warm like the sun shining on a white sandy beach. He'd already pictured her naked more times than he could count. At first he'd tried to stop himself, but then he just indulged. Now he couldn't stop, and he'd started adding details he was eager to verify. This was not good. Women had never been a strong point for him. Facts, statistics, hypotheses he could grasp. But the female mind was a mystery. With three older sisters it wouldn't seem so, but they'd been more like aunts than siblings. They were older and nurturing of the youngest and only boy in the family.

In his career, he felt safe. Now Lora had taken that safety from him. He couldn't predict her. She was like a wild variable in a controlled experiment. Why did she have to change her hair? He couldn't stop staring at the golden highlights that glistened when she moved. He noticed how strands brushed against her neck. It was very distracting.

He knew she hated him and he wanted to change that, but she always met any attempt at a truce with suspicion. He'd just have to try harder. He couldn't make her forget the past, but perhaps he could get her to forgive him. Hell, he shouldn't even care. He didn't want to. After all, she wasn't just a personal threat, but also a professional one. Lora was a viable opponent in the race for the Poindexter Fellowship, and he had to make sure that he kept his record in place. That's what he needed to focus on. Not a pair of beautiful brown eyes he wanted to see dilate with desire, or soft full lips he wanted to taste.

Justin glanced out the window. It was a bright, sunny day, but it didn't disguise the late November chill. People were bundled up as they marched down the street. Holiday wreaths decorated buildings, and strings of colored lights draped around the trees, ready to light the darkness when evening came. Ah, he loved the holidays. He was looking forward to his nieces' holiday pageant, the food, the gift giving and spending time with his family. They were the only people who seemed to understand him and with whom he could be himself and relax.

But this year would be different; he had to up his game for the fellowship, which meant spending long days and nights, and even weekends, in the lab. His poor dog, Louis, a three-year-old American bulldog, was showing signs of frustration from not having him around. The past two evenings Justin had come home to a house full of shredded paper. Louis had gotten into his study and emptied his trash bin. But for now, he couldn't worry about his dog—he had something more urgent to worry about. Yes, he'd forget about Lora Rice. He had to.

Oh, how she hated the holidays. It was the last week of November, and holiday madness had begun. Lora navigated her way through the crowded mall, regretting her decision to help her older sister, Belinda, go shopping. Her sister seemed to have an ever-growing list of people she had to shop for.

When they were kids Lora had nicknamed her "The Bullet" because sometimes she could hit you right between the eyes with a tactless remark or demand. Her sister was beautiful and knew it, and she took advantage of her looks to get her way. She had one failed marriage behind her and was already planning for husband number two.

"Can you make it to my party?" Belinda asked, handing Lora another bag to carry while she studied the mall map.

"I have a cold."

Belinda looked at her sister, unconvinced. "You don't have a cold."

Lora rubbed her throat. "I feel one coming on."

"You had a cold last year."

"It's coming back."

"And the year before that."

Lora shrugged. "What can I say? I'm susceptible."

"To the same cold around the same time each year? Come on, you'll have fun."

"No, thanks. You know I hate the holidays."

"Still? I thought you'd gotten over that. I know as kids we didn't have many happy memories, especially around the holidays, but we can make up for it now."

"By drinking with a bunch of strangers?"

"They're friends."

"Your friends. Sorry, but my schedule is full." *Full of false cheer,* she thought. She didn't look forward to the office party or her parents' holiday gathering or her grandmother's holiday dinner, where she'd be asked again and again if she was seeing someone. She didn't want to add Belinda's bash on top of them. She wanted this holiday season to be different. Something had to change.

"I won't take 'no' for an answer," Belinda said. "You have to come, or I'll get Mom to force you."

Lora inwardly shivered. Whereas her sister was like a bullet, her mother was like a pair of handcuffs. Once she locked into you, you couldn't escape. "Okay, you're right," Lora said quickly. "I wasn't being honest with you."

"I knew it."

"I have a date," she said, hoping her lie sounded convincing.

Belinda frowned. "With a man?"

Lora nudged Belinda with her elbow, affronted. "Of course with a man."

"Not necessarily. Knowing you, you could be talking about a rat or monkey."

"My experiments don't involve animals."

"What's his name?"

"Just somebody at work. What's the next store?" Lora asked.

"Who?" Belinda pressed.

Lora adjusted one of the five shopping bags she was carrying, feeling like a beast of burden. "If it works out, you'll know."

Belinda tapped her chin, looking intrigued. She was only carrying two bags because she said she needed to keep her hands free to hold the map and organize their shopping expedition. "You never talk about the people at your workplace except that guy you hate, Dr. Sliver."

"Silver," Lora corrected.

"Whatever. So what makes this guy so special?"

"When you meet him you'll know."

"Let's double date."

"No."

"But I'm curious. This is your first date in—" She stopped. "Wait…have you ever had a first date?"

"Of course."

"No, I mean a date you got on your own. Not one set up by me or Mom or Uncle Rudy."

Lora curled her lip. "Never mention that again."

"His heart was in the right place."

"Maybe, but I don't know where he'd put his brain." Her uncle Rudy, her mother's brother, had set her up on a date with a dock worker forty years her senior, whose main topic of conversation was his low libido and fear of dying alone.

"That was a mistake I'll *never* repeat."

"So this isn't a blind date?"

"No." Lora gestured to one of the window displays. "Doesn't that dress look like something perfect for someone on your list?"

Belinda ignored her. "Did he ask you out, or did *you* ask *him?*"

"It was sort of mutual." At least that's how she hoped it would be one day.

"I want to hear all about this mystery man after your date."

"You will."

"And he had better be real."

Oh, he was real all right. He just hadn't noticed her yet. When she'd first laid eyes on Dr. Warren T. Rappaport, she'd had to stop herself from staring. She soon discovered that not only was he good looking, with rich caramel skin and chestnut eyes, but he also laughed easily, had a warm smile and always had a kind word. But the best part was the fact that he was single.

Suddenly, Lora spotted him only a few feet away, as if just by thinking of him she'd conjured him up.

She had to act fast or he'd be gone. She waved. She didn't expect him to see her at first, but he waved back and then started toward them. If her arms hadn't been loaded down with bags she would have clutched her chest. *Remember to breathe. Remember to breathe.*

"Hi Lora," he said.

"Hi. This is my sister, Belinda."

"A pleasure to meet you. I see good looks run in the family."

"And you are?" Belinda went into her "do you see me" mode. She wasn't used to being ignored, and Rappaport was surprisingly focused on Lora.

"Sorry," Lora said, ashamed that she hadn't introduced him. "This is Dr. Warren Rappaport."

"There's quite a crowd here today," Warren said. "I was just going to escape the madness by getting something to drink. Care to join me?"

Belinda shook her head. "I wish we could, but we have loads more shopping to do."

"Can't we finish it another day?" Lora said under her breath.

"No."

"I'll call you."

"But I'm your ride."

"I'll find my way home," Lora said, sending Warren a quick glance. She knew he could hear them.

Belinda made a face. "You said you'd help me."

Lora clenched her teeth. "I'll make it up to you."

"Is he the one you have a—"

"I'll tell you later."

Belinda shot Warren a suspicious glance, then grabbed some of Lora's bags. "All right. Be careful and call me when you get home." She kissed her sister on the cheek. "Nice to meet you, Warren," she said as she walked off.

Warren looped Lora's arm through his. "I thought she'd never leave. Is she always that overprotective?"

"She likes to look out for me." Lora said, pleased by his charm.

They took the escalator to the third floor and went to the food court, where they were fortunate enough to find a table currently being vacated by a group of teenagers. He asked her what she wanted, then left to get the beverages.

"It's been a crazy day shopping," he said, returning with a plate of chips with nacho cheese and two drinks.

"I do most of my shopping online, but Belinda dragged me here."

He grinned. "I'm glad she did."

Lora sipped her drink, feeling her face grow warm. "It must not be like home," she said, trying to recover. Warren had transferred from a small town in Georgia, and it seemed like he hadn't gotten used to the big city yet.

"No. I had to fight with somebody for Digital Dilly."

She adjusted her glasses. "Digital what?"

"It's this new robotic horse that's all the craze with little girls. You can feed it and take care of it and play games with it on your computer. I wanted to get it for my young cousin who's sick, but this guy beat me to it. Although I offered him double the price and told him why I wanted it, he refused. He said he wanted it for his beloved niece and nothing could change his mind."

"Some people are so selfish."

Warren dipped a chip into the cheese and sighed. "I didn't expect it from him. But I guess I should have."

"Why?"

"Because…" He stopped, ate his chip, then reached for his drink. "Never mind. I shouldn't have said anything."

"Why?" Lora asked, now even more intrigued. "What won't you tell me?"

"Because you know him. We both do."

"Really? Who is it?"

"Silver."

"What? He's here? In the mall? I never thought of him participating in normal activities like shopping in a mall."

"Yep, he can be ordinary sometimes, but he's a hard bastard to bargain with."

"I know," Lora said. Although this was worse than even she had imagined. Why couldn't he give up a toy for a sick little girl?

"Uh, oh."

"What?"

"I really shouldn't have said anything," Warren said, lowering his head and lifting his hand to hide his face.

"Why?"

"Guess who's coming our way."

Chapter 2

"Hello, Rice. Didn't expect to see you here."

There was nothing warm about his greeting. It was just a series of stated facts, but somehow it was unnerving. He always unnerved her, and she didn't know why. He looked more relaxed and less threatening out of his white lab coat, wearing a pair of dark blue jeans and a black leather jacket. Damn, he was a good-looking man. Lora had always suspected it, but now it was even more evident. She caught a woman sending him a glance. She didn't blame her— she would have done the same if she didn't know what he was really like. She plastered on a smile.

"I see you've been shopping," Lora said, just to fill the silence.

"Yes." He lifted the bag, as if in triumph. "My niece wanted this popular toy, and I was able to snag it for her."

Lora glanced at Warren, who still hadn't raised his head. Because he wouldn't mention the incident, she would. Silver had no right to look so proud. "And there's another little girl who won't get it. But perhaps you don't think she needs it."

He furrowed his brows. "What?"

"I just heard about what you did."

"I don't understand."

"Let me clarify." Warren lifted his head. "Hey, Silver."

"Rappaport," he said, his tone turning to ice. "Still charming the ladies with stories, I see."

"It's what I do." He motioned to a chair. "Care to join us?"

"I have more shopping to do."

"And more presents to *take,*" Lora added.

Silver sent her an odd look—a mixture of confusion and disappointment—which for a second made her regret her petty words. But she quickly brushed the feeling aside. She had nothing to feel sorry for. She knew he was a bully who liked to get his own way, and she knew how he really felt about the sick. They were merely "experimental" lab specimens to him. She'd seen his callousness in the past. She didn't even know why he was still working in medical research. He could get better paid positions elsewhere. Perhaps he just liked the prestige.

"I'll see you," he said frowning, then left.

"I seriously hope not," she muttered, wishing the restless feeling that had seized her would leave. Silver had a strong visceral effect on her that she couldn't understand.

Warren gave a low whistle once Silver was out of view. "I'd hate to get on your bad side. I see you dislike Silver as much as I do. What's your story?"

It was too personal to share. "A personality clash."

"I can see that, but people usually overlook it."

"Why?"

"He's a brilliant man."

Lora played with the straw in her drink, drawing it up and down so it squeaked. "He's all mind and no heart."

"That sounds serious. Were you two lovers or something?"

Lora stared at him, outraged. "Absolutely not. Why would you suggest something like that?"

Warren shrugged. "I don't know. There just seems to be this energy between you two, as if you have a history."

"We have a history but not as lovers."

"And you're not ready to tell me about it?"

"Not yet."

Warren winked. "I like a woman of mystery."

"Good, because I have plenty of secrets."

Warren folded his arms and studied her for a moment, then said, "Have you ever met his family?"

"Why would I want to?"

"So is that a no?"

"A definite no. Have you?"

"Yes." He leaned forward, resting his arms on the table. "His whole family is that way—proud, arrogant and determined."

"That's no surprise."

"His niece is the worst. She's spoiled, vain but brilliant and condescending to anyone who she thinks is inferior."

"How do you know so much? How did you meet them?"

"I did an extended study after graduate school, and Silver and I shared a room. I thought he was okay at first, until he got me kicked out of the program because I won an award he wanted."

"He got you thrown out? How could he do that?"

"He had connections and a vindictive streak. I'm telling you this so you'll watch out. It's not good to aggravate him, no matter how much he annoys you. Don't get on his bad side."

"Too late." Lora shook her head, amazed. "How can you stand to see him every day?"

"He can't really touch me, so there's no threat. Dr. Yung loves my work and he's been at Ventico a lot longer than Silver. Although Silver is the director, he doesn't mess with Dr. Yung for one main reason—his research is the largest and most lucrative of the three projects. And he has seniority and some powerful allies in Washington.

"So I guess your evaluation was better than mine."

"Depends."

"He doesn't like my methods. He said I was *undisciplined* and tended to 'jump to conclusions.'"

"Yes, that's Silver for you. Every statement you make must be backed up with undeniable proof. He doesn't seem to understand that science also has an element of art and instinct."

"Exactly."

"It's nice to meet a like-minded colleague. We'll

change the world and leave the others behind. Just stay close to me—I won't steer you wrong."

Lora planned to stay close. Very close. Her face flushed as she briefly thought of them in a romantic embrace, lying naked together on her queen-size bed with rose petals sprinkled all around. She shook the fantasy off and regained her composure. "Thanks for the drink and the nachos. It was nice."

"We should do this again. Perhaps in a place less noisy and crowded."

Yes, like my place or yours. "I'd like that," she said, hoping she didn't sound too giddy.

"Me, too. Call me." He gave her his number, flashed a heart-melting smile, then left.

Lora hummed all the way home, and when she exited the taxi, she gave the driver a large tip and wished him "Happy Holidays," which she never did. Yes, this holiday would be different. This year she wouldn't be shy and alone. She'd found the right guy, and it would stop her family from setting her up or feeling sorry for her. She now had Warren's interest—and his cell number. It was time for Chapter 4: Catching His Attention and Chapter 5: Reeling Him In. She was ready to put her plan into action and win his heart.

If Warren was a man who smoked, he'd light up a cigarette. As he walked away from Lora, he realized that he felt better than he had in years. He was going to have a lot of fun with her. He needed some excitement, and she was just the type of woman to give it to him. It wasn't easy to find a woman who despised Silver as much as he did. It had been bad luck that he'd ended up at Ventico and under Silver's watch again. But this time, he wouldn't be vulnerable. And working with Dr. Yung provided him the protection he needed. If he played his cards right, he'd rule that place one day. Getting to where he wanted to be was number one. And he now knew that Lora was the key. He'd use her to put Silver exactly where he wanted him.

Lora and Rappaport! Justin marched through the parking lot as the sight of the pair burned in his mind. He gripped his shopping bags until their plastic handles bit into his palm. He should've guessed. Rappaport always had the good fortune of showing up in the right place at the right time. It was a talent of his. Justin piled his purchases into the trunk of his car, his sense of victory now gone. He'd gotten the toy for his niece, Monique, but he may have lost the woman he wanted. Not that he'd ever had her, but he'd been hopeful. Justin slammed the trunk shut, then got inside his car and headed to his office. He could think clearer there. This wasn't the outcome he'd pictured when he'd first spotted Lora sitting in the crowded food court.

He'd felt his pulse pick up speed but didn't care as he watched her happy and inviting smile. He imagined buying her a drink, telling her about his niece and maybe asking her out. He hadn't noticed the man sitting at the table until he was almost upon her, and he'd foolishly thought he was a brother or a cousin because he knew she was single. Then Rappaport had turned with the same smug look Justin remembered, and he'd seen how Lora's happiness had disappeared. Not because of Rappaport, but because of him. She'd never looked at him with any warmth or joy. He'd hoped to change that, but obviously that wouldn't be today. It didn't matter. This was good; he shouldn't think of her that way anyway. He needed to remember that she was his competition.

He wasn't concerned about working late in the office. There was no one at home worrying or waiting for him. He'd already fed and walked Louis, so he knew he'd be fine for the night.

A half hour later he sat in his lab and glanced over his notes. He'd hit a wall in his research, which was unusual for him. Some of what he was doing was more speculative than factual, and he needed to find and add more proof to back up his hypothesis. He knew it would be worth it in the end but, at that moment, he wasn't sure which direction he wanted to go. He'd been working for almost an hour when he heard a knock on the door. "Come in."

"This is not good."

Justin smiled at the man who'd entered. He looked like a misplaced librarian who should be surrounded by books instead of lab equipment. He kept his glasses pushed up over his gray and thinning hair. Dr. Oliver Rollins, who also worked at Ventico, was a renowned scientist from the UK who was both a mentor and a friend, even though he was twenty years his senior. "Nice to see you, too."

"You can't push like this."

"I have to."

"You know your health is more important than a competition."

"You don't have to worry about me." Oliver was one of the few people who knew all about him. At times it was a relief, but at times like this, it was a burden. Justin didn't want anyone to use his health as a reason he shouldn't do what he wanted to. He didn't want pity or concern. As a child he was diagnosed with moderate to severe sickle cell anemia, and at nine, he'd had to have his spleen removed. It had been diseased from a shortage of oxygen during one of his many pain crises. In elementary school, although his parents were extremely worried and overprotective, he was determined to participate in sports. As a result, he experienced several pain crises and had to be put on strong pain pills. One of the side effects was that he fell asleep often, and by the time he was in high school, the few friends he had thought he was taking drugs. That's what he hated most growing up— being extremely tired and in extreme pain. But he kept it hidden so no one ever saw him in agony.

The painful crises lasted from 7 to 10 days, and often took about a week for him to recuperate and get back his strength. The hardest part was wondering when another crisis would occur and realizing that, no matter what medication they gave him, the pain would always come back. It felt like being stabbed with a knife in the same place, over and over again. During one particularly brutal month, he had had more than three blood transfusions. As a result, he'd lost a lot of time from school and had to be tutored at home. Fortunately, he was swift and academically inclined and stayed on top of his courses. Being the only person in his whole family with the disease made him feel felt like an outsider.

"I know how to take care of myself," he said.

Oliver tapped the table. "You haven't in the past couple years. Your life has only been your work."

"I'm a passionate man."

"Who's living a passionless life. When's the last time you've been with a woman?"

Justin looked at him, stunned. "Oliver."

His friend shrugged and tapped his chest. "I'm a man. You're a man. This is not a hard question to answer."

"I don't have time for this kind of talk."

"Justin, you won't live forever. Make time. You need the soft feel of a woman's touch. Her warm embrace."

Justin laughed. "Do you have someone in mind?"

"No, but if you want…"

"I was joking."

"This is not a joking matter. I am serious. You're a good man. I don't want to see you alone."

"I'm not alone. I have my family."

"I remember you once saying you wanted a family of your own."

"That was when I was young and naive."

"You're still young."

"Not young enough to be naive. Let's talk about something more interesting."

"What's more interesting than this?"

"Actually—"

"That was a rhetorical question."

"I tried a relationship, remember? It didn't work out."

Justin had been working at the Johns Hopkins University Medical School as a research fellow when he'd met Devina. She was of African-Mediterranean descent, and although not a great beauty, she was very bright. It was love at first sight. Because of his illness, he had never really dated in high school and college—which didn't mean he hadn't gone out with girls. Quite the opposite. The girls asked him out, and his sisters and parents were always fielding calls from one girl or another. But he had never fallen in love or anything even close. With Devina, it had been different.

On their first date he had taken her to see the Alvin Ailey dance troupe at the Kennedy Center. Before long, she was spending nights at his place and their relationship blossomed. Then it happened. He suffered a major crisis and spent two weeks in the hospital. Devina came to visit him the first day he was admitted, but after that she was gone. Oliver had never liked her and had told Justin to be careful, but he hadn't listened. His sisters also didn't take to her, but by the time he realized the kind of person she was, she'd left. He never saw her again.

Six months later, he saw an article in a newspaper announcing the appointment of Dr. Devina Davis as director of research at Abbot Labs. It was then Justin realized she had conned him. They had been extremely close, and he'd shared some of his research with her, including the white paper he hadn't submitted yet for publication. The article mentioned Dr.

Davis's research: stem-cell theory and the cellular manifestation of abnormal hemoglobin. It was the title of his research project. She had stolen his work. No, Devina had been enough of an experience. "This is the best life for me," he said.

Oliver brushed the thought aside with a quick flick of his wrist. "She was nothing. I told you she was a user and wrong for you, but you didn't listen. She said things that were not true. I don't know everything, but I do know this." He pointed at Justin. "There is a woman out there for you, and I plan to dance at your wedding."

Justin grinned. "That I'd like to see."

"And you will. I love you like a son. I want to see you happy."

"I am happy. I will be happier when I win the fellowship."

"You've already won it twice."

"I want it again."

Oliver threw up his hands. "Why? Your reputation is stellar. You could work in any lab you choose. You've been quoted and printed in all the leading science journals, and you serve on the board of two nationally recognized science organizations. You sold a science patent to Siesmen for nearly a million dollars, and even though you gave the proceeds to research I know you still get royalties. You've achieved more than most men do in their entire lifetime. You don't need another trophy."

"I like to win."

"Even if you win, it won't be enough. It will be a hollow victory. You need a life."

"I have a life—my family and my work. It suits me. It always has, and it always will."

"You've given up on women?"

"No."

"Yes, you have, and that's why you're here locked away."

Justin shook his head. "No, that's not it. I just needed to get away and think."

"About what? What's bothering you?"

Justin sighed. "There is a woman but…forget it."

Oliver's eyes brightened. "Really? You're interested in someone? Who is she? What's her name? Do I know her?"

Yes, he did know her, but Oliver didn't need to know that. "There's a problem."

"She's married?"

"She hates me."

Oliver waved his hand, annoyed. "Then she's a stupid woman, and you're better off without her."

"Exactly, which is why I am here."

Oliver folded his arms. "Forget this woman and find another. There are so many." A sly grin spread across his face. "If I were your age and had that face of yours, I'd hardly be in the office, and every morning I'd have bags under my eyes." He snapped his fingers. "Actually, there is this one woman in particular that Anya has been eyeing for you."

Justin laughed. "For how long?"

"A couple of months. She met her at one of her grief counseling sessions." Oliver's wife, Anya, had started attending the group after the death of their three-year-old granddaughter from a rare form of leukemia. "She says the woman is smart, kind and in her thirties, the right age for marriage and children."

"I'll be lucky if I make it to forty."

Oliver's tone hardened. "You promised me never to speak like that again. You will live a long, full life."

"I'm sorry," Justin said quickly. He hated to see his friend upset. "Okay, what's her name?"

"They don't share real names in the group to keep a sense of anonymity, so, Anya calls her Lillian."

Justin poured apple juice from his thermos, then took a long swallow. A date would be something to distract him from thinking of Lora. What was the harm? "If she's willing to meet me, I'm open."

Oliver beamed and patted him on the back. "Good boy. That's my Justin. You'll really like her. Just remember to be a bit more..." He searched for words.

"What?"

"Gracious."

"I am gracious."

"Tactful then. At times you can be too 'to the point' with people."

"I like to be honest."

"You can be honest without being inconsiderate. Those who know you understand you, but to others..."

"I'm a cold bastard. I know what they say. I'm not going to soften my words because people have self-esteem issues. I'm running a lab, not a kindergarten class. And when it comes to women, I don't believe in false flattery."

"You'll have to soften your stance for the right woman, and she'll be worth it."

"Have you met her?"

"No, but from everything Anya has said, you'll like her. Also, we have a great gift for you this holiday. Remember that party I told you we're having this Saturday?"

"Yes."

"We're expecting quite a crowd, so we rented a hall for the event. There'll be great food, live music and great company. I want to see you there. Let's head out now, and I'll tell you more. You need to eat."

"I'll take a rain check."

"Promise to work no more than an hour."

"Okay."

"I'll be back to check."

"I know."

Once Oliver had gone Justin sat back in his chair, no longer able to focus on work. His friend wanted him to have the life he had stopped hoping for. But perhaps he could hope again. Perhaps he could let himself dream about having a family of his own. He could imagine his home filled with the scent of his wife's perfume and the bright smile of a son and daughter greeting him at the door. He'd take them on vacations to the beach and holidays in the South Seas. Perhaps this would be a true season of miracles. He thought of Lora and Rappaport. The image of them together still stung, but his friend had given him something else to think about. It was then, at that moment, that he realized he would give up the Pointdexter Fellowship and all it promised, if it meant he could have the right woman by his side.

* * *

As she sat in the circle, Lora wondered if she was finally ready to move on from grief counseling. The meetings had helped her cope with Suzette's death three years ago, and she did feel stronger.

The holidays were always hard for her. It was as if they magnified every pain, every heartbreak, but somehow this year, for the first time, she felt as if she could survive. She felt as if she could be happy again, live again. She knew that's what Suzette would have wanted. After returning home from the mall and calling her sister, she'd been surprised that her thoughts hadn't gone to Warren but rather Silver. He seemed to always fuel her into action. Justin made her angry, and somehow she welcomed it because he was the one person who continued to make her feel. Before him she had stopped feeling, ever since Suzette's death from sickle cell anemia. She'd buried herself in her work and had been sleepwalking through life until she'd seen Justin Silver again over a year ago. Just seeing him filled her with fire, and it was both a pain and pleasure. No other person could make her react as he did, but it was good because it forced her to feel. It forced her to act.

She would beat him in the competition, and then she'd transfer to another lab while putting her love life in order. She knew Warren was the perfect choice. She no longer wanted to grieve—she wanted to rejoice.

At the end of the counseling meeting a short, silver-haired lady she called Annabel came up to her. She always looked ready for a good time, as if she'd host a tea party with cups filled with gin. "You're look-ing pretty today," she said. "What's the occasion?"

"It's part of my plan."

"Plan?"

"Yes. I've been reading this book called *30 Days to Romance*."

Anya pinched her lips as if she'd tasted something sour. "A book?"

"What's wrong with a book?"

"Nothing, it's just…why didn't you tell me you wanted romance? A book can't tell you anything about men that I don't already know. If you want a man, just say the word."

"I already have one in mind."

"So do I. And I bet you my choice is better than yours."

Lora giggled at the thought of her friend setting her up. "Mine is successful, funny and handsome."

"So is mine, but he is also very kind and consider-ate. He's thirty-six and never married, but he wants to be, and he treats his family well."

"He sounds like the ideal man."

Anya grinned. "Curious?"

"Definitely."

Annabel clasped her hands together. "Good. This is what I'll do. I'm hosting a party this Saturday, and I'll introduce you then."

Lora remembered Annabel handing her the in-vitation two weeks ago, but she hadn't responded. "I'll be there."

Lora left the meeting wanting to sing despite the bitter cold brushing her face and the bare trees shivering in the light breeze. Could it be this easy? Would she really find a match this year? She trusted her friend. She was always honest and had helped Lora through some of the dark days following Suzette's death. Now was the time for hope and light. Yes, she was ready to live again and find love. After all, it had been more than three years since she'd met Justin Silver, who'd attracted and repelled her on the same day.

Chapter 3

Three years ago

She had just gotten a call from Suzette's mother that Suzette was going downhill fast. Lora grabbed her jacket and car keys and was out the door in less than a minute. As she drove to the National Institute of Health in Bethesda, Maryland, Lora could barely focus. She was totally unaware that she was going sixty miles per hour in a thirty-five-miles-per-hour zone. All she could focus on was the fact that she wanted her friend to live. What would she do without her? They had known each other since first grade. It had been an instant friendship. They were both new to the school and the area, and they were both first generation, born in the United States to immigrant parents. Suzette was the third child born to parents

from Spain and Italy and she had not been screened
at birth. It was only by accident, when she had had a
crisis and had gone to a hospital, that the emergency
room doctor tested her for sickle cell anemia. That
was when she discovered she had the disease.

Before then, and unfortunately afterward, whenever she had a crisis and turned up in an emergency
room, she faced doctors who thought she was just a
junkie wanting to get high on pain killers. They never
considered that a fair-haired, blue-eyed young woman
would have sickle cell anemia.

Lora was shy, and some of the kids had picked
on her, but Suzette had instantly taken Lora under
her wing and was always there to speak up for her.
They had fun sleeping over at each other's house and
having picnics in the backyard with their dolls and
stuffed toys. But, although there were the good times,
Lora also remembered her friend being ill from time
to time and having to miss days from school. Thankfully, Suzette's mother let Lora visit her at home, but
there were times all her friend could do was lie on
the couch. Through elementary and middle school
she had watched Suzette get sick, but no one knew
why until she was diagnosed with sickle cell anemia
when she was in her first year at college.

No, her friend could not—would not—die.

As she drove up to the hospital, Lora felt a sicken-
ing feeling in her stomach. She put up a small prayer.
"God, please, please, don't take Suzette from me."
Then she entered the hospital, signed in and raced to
the tertiary unit. Suzette had been transferred there
overnight. When Lora entered Suzette's room she saw

a lonely figure sitting beside her bed. Mrs. Gannotti, Suzette's mother, had short reddish-brown hair and green eyes, which were red and puffy from crying. She'd divorced Suzette's father shortly after Suzette was born, and he had never kept in touch with his daughter. Mrs. Gannotti had never remarried, and Suzette was her only daughter. Lora could see the devastation on her face.

Lora walked over to the bed. Suzette lay still, her face ashen and drawn. As Lora got closer, Suzette turned, looked up at her and barely managed a smile; her blue eyes had lost their bright spark, and her blond hair lay limp on the pillow.

Lora took her hand. "What handsome doctor's attention are you trying to get with all this drama?"

"I'm so tired," she said in a hoarse whisper.

"I know, but you have to get better. Are you in pain?"

"No."

"You've fought this before, and you will again."

Suzette's eyes welled with tears. "I don't think I'll make it this time."

Lora swallowed, struggling to keep her own tears at bay, her heart constricting with pain. "It's going to be all right." She turned, hoping Mrs. Gannotti would agree. She remained mute, but her eyes showed her fear. Before she could say any more, a group of doctors entered the room.

"Good morning, Mrs. Gannotti," said a tall skinny man leading the group. Lora recognized him as Suzette's physician, Dr. Monroe. "How did she sleep last night?"

After Mrs. Gannotti answered, Dr. Monroe turned and discussed Suzette's case with the group of white coats. Lora noticed another man, not just because he was the only black man in the group or even because he was exceedingly handsome. She noticed him because he didn't seem to have the clinical distance the other residents had. Actually, he didn't look like a resident at all; he looked aware and tuned-in. She looked at his badge: Dr. Justin Silver. She saw his gaze drift to Suzette, compassion apparent in his eyes. Lora could tell that he didn't just see Suzette as a patient or a disease to be analyzed; he saw her as a person. She wanted to tell him all about Suzette. That she liked eating hot-fudge sundaes sprinkled with nuts and going to live stage musicals, and that they planned to go to Aruba one day. That her friend was the reason Lora had decided to make sickle cell research her focus.

Instead, she watched Dr. Monroe finish his talk, take a cursory look over Suzette's medical chart, then send a significant look to Dr. Silver. Dr. Monroe smiled and said goodbye, and the group left. Lora stroked Suzette's hand for a moment, then turned and went into the bathroom off of her room just to breathe. She had to be strong for her friend and Mrs. Gannotti. As she headed out of the bathroom, through the half-opened door she heard Dr. Monroe's voice coming from just outside Suzette's room. "What do you think about the Gannotti case?"

She peeked her head around the corner and saw him speaking to Dr. Silver.

"The same as I did the first time," Dr. Silver said

in a flat tone. "You told me about her. Her case is too far gone for the treatment I've been working on. She's going to die, so this is the best place for her. Just keep her comfortable and let nature take its course." He rested his hands on his hips. "We shouldn't have wasted time."

"Her mother didn't agree to her being in a trial, but I spoke to her friend Lora, and she thought there may still be a chance that—"

"I don't care what a grief-stricken, half-delusional friend thinks or has to say about this case." Dr. Silver folded his arms and shook his head in disgust. "This is the consequence of her mother's decision, and now we get blamed for her condition."

Lora's temper flared. Who was this man? The Angel of Death, selecting who should live and who should die? She knew it was best not to get involved, but she couldn't pretend she hadn't overheard what they'd said. She stepped around the corner and faced them.

"You heartless, unfeeling toad."

"Lora—" Dr. Monroe said.

"How dare you consider my friend a waste of time."

Dr. Silver's hands fell to his sides. "I didn't say that."

"Why won't you let her try your treatment?"

"Lora," Dr. Monroe said, "it's too late. We've done all that we can. Suzette is not going to be able to pull through this time."

"You think you know everything, but it took nearly eighteen years to diagnosis her with sickle cell." During this most recent crisis, the hospital she had been taken to at first had not looked for sickle cell until it was too late because she'd forgotten to wear her medical alert bracelet. This time she'd suffered a major crisis, robbing her vital organs of needed oxygen, and some of her organs were now too damaged to repair.

"What could Mrs. Gannotti do? Her only daughter isn't some lab rat for you to experiment on. And she's my friend. You talk about consequences, but what do you know about her? She has lived with this disease for her entire twenty-nine years, enduring all the painful episodes and hospitalizations. But she loves life and wants to live. I can see it in her eyes. What's too late? Is it too late to have compassion? Is it too late to give her mother some hope? Suzette is all she has. Do you know why her mother refused to enroll her in your clinical trial? Did anyone ask, or were you too busy condemning her to death?

"Mrs. Gannotti's grandfather had been in a clinical trial, back home in Spain, that tortured him. So you see, it was *never* too late, it was just that none of you cared enough to really discover why she wouldn't put her daughter in your trial. And none of you cared enough to explain the process to her. You didn't care to ask the right questions."

"Well there's nothing we can do now," Dr. Monroe replied.

"To think I actually thought you were looking at my friend with empathy. One day I'll make you both regret your decision."

Neither doctor said anything.

Suzette died that day.

* * *

As Lora walked to her apartment, she remembered her vow. But now was not the time to be sad—now was a time for hope. She wiped her tears and opened her door. Her cell phone buzzed just as she was hanging up her coat. She glanced at it and saw a blocked number and then a photo of an elegant restaurant. The text below it read:

How does an expensive Japanese dinner sound?
Warren

Lora did a little dance then texted him back:

Sounds great.

Pick u up on Saturday.

This Saturday? The same Saturday as Annabel's party? Lora groaned. Should she cancel? A part of her wanted to, but another part was curious about the man Annabel wanted her to meet. She texted back:

Make it next Saturday.

Okay, c u then.

Lora skipped around her apartment, then fell into her couch and let out a mini scream of delight. Dinner with Warren. Perfect!

That Saturday, still floating from Warren's recent text, Lora asked her sister to help her get ready for Annabel's party. The moment her sister came through the door carrying a large case of makeup Lora realized she'd made a mistake.

"But I can't wear all that," Lora said as Belinda began making up her face.

"Hush. I've been waiting years for this moment. Your face has been dying for the right cosmetics."

Her sister finished styling her hair, which she pulled into an upswept cluster of curls with a thin bang. "Wow, I hadn't noticed you got your hair highlighted," she said.

Finally, someone other than Silver noticed, Lora thought. Belinda placed a small suitcase on the bed and pulled out a cute knee-length black dress with a scooped neckline. Lora put it on nervously.

"But the neckline falls too low," Lora complained, trying to pull the front of the dress higher.

"Don't be such a prude. You've got a great figure, and it's time you showed it off."

"I'm not being a prude—I just don't want to come across looking like a call girl."

"Please, that won't happen. The dress fits you perfectly and showing a little skin will help."

Lora secretly decided she'd use a couple of safety pins once her sister left.

To add some color, Belinda added a thin red silk fringed shawl, just in case Lora got chilly. To finish off the look, she loaned Lora a pair of black suede wedges. Once finished, Belinda stepped back and clapped her hands, delighted. "My masterpiece."

Lora turned to look at her image in the full-length mirror and bit back a scream.

"I look like a freak show!"

"No, you don't."

"My hair is too high, and my makeup is too strong."

"No, it's not. You should always wear heavier makeup for an evening event. You're the one who called me over to help you," she said in a hurt voice.

Lora held back a swear word. This was her fault, not Belinda's. She turned and hugged her sister. "Thank you."

"Have a great time."

Lora forced a smile. "I will," she said, hoping the lights at the party would be dim.

"Tie or no tie?" Justin held up both items for his dog, Louis, to see. He'd only had his new companion for a year.

"We're sending you a special surprise," his mother had told him one autumn morning. "It'll arrive in a day or two." His parents had just arrived back home in Oregon after one of their rare visits to see him. While staying with him they had complained on and off that they didn't like him living alone. No matter how much he told them that he had work to keep him busy and great colleagues to work with, they were scared about something happening to him. They especially worried about who would take care of him, even though his three sisters lived close by.

Justin had sighed, in no mood for what his mother was planning. "I don't want a surprise…just tell me what it is."

"No, but it's just what you need," she had said, and he had heard his father snickering in the background.

Justin hadn't been able to guess what his parents

were up to. Two days later he had received a knock on the door—the delivery of a two-year-old American bulldog. His first instinct had been to reject it. He was a busy man and didn't have time for a puppy. But then Louis did something that stole his heart. He didn't lick him—he sneezed and then wagged his tail as if he were the happiest animal alive. Justin thought it was such a funny sight, and he knew that the puppy would stay. Getting used to having a dog wouldn't be difficult. He'd had a golden retriever growing up, and they were inseparable until it had died of old age. After that, he couldn't bring himself to get another dog because he didn't want to experience that kind of loss again.

Louis changed his mind. After that initial meeting the two of them hit it off. He named him Louis, after Louis Pasteur, and from the first day, he let him sleep in his bedroom with him.

Although he was still young, Louis was trained and would respond to most of Justin's orders. One order he never listened to, however, was to stay off the couch. Nothing bothered Justin more than having dog hair all over the place. He didn't mind it on the rugs, but the couch and his bed were off-limits for Louis. But, although he never saw him go on either piece of furniture when he was home, Justin had a sinking feeling that Louis did go on the forbidden cozy spots once he was gone. Louis was clever to never get caught.

Justin looked at his clever dog now. Louis stared back at him, as if he were truly contemplating whether his owner should wear a tie or not.

Justin looked at the options in his hand. "It's supposed to be casual, but I'm not sure. So what do you think?"

Before Justin could answer his own question, the doorbell rang. He glanced at his watch. He wasn't expecting visitors, and he didn't have much time before he needed to leave. He opened the door and saw two of his sisters—Maureen and Sarah—standing there. Maureen was the eldest of the three and took her role seriously. She had the sturdy bearing of a drill sergeant with her short cropped hairstyle, and she often dressed in all black. His middle sister, Sarah, was more fun-loving, as exemplified by her outfit of an oversize blouse and floor-length peasant skirt.

"You're not wearing that," Maureen said, marching through the door.

Justin looked down at his clothes. "What's wrong with it?"

"There's not enough time to tell you."

Sarah patted him on the arm. "Anya called us to make sure you looked your best."

"But—"

Maureen pointed to his bedroom. "Don't argue, just move."

Justin knew if he didn't want to be late he'd better keep his mouth shut. He sat on the bed while his sisters sifted through his closet.

"We're really glad you're doing this," Sarah said.

"Letting you hijack my life?"

"No, meeting a woman."

"Anya told us everything," Maureen said. "This woman sounds great." She lifted a decorative shirt.

"I'm not wearing that," Justin said.

"You never wear it!"

"I know. I keep it because it was a gift, but I'd rather go bare-chested than in something like that."

Sarah tapped her chin thoughtfully. "That would be a good idea. You should flaunt what you have."

"You're embarrassing him."

She pinched his cheeks. "Am I, little brother?"

He brushed her hand away. "Watch yourself or I'll stop being nice."

She laughed, then returned to the closet. Minutes later they were done dressing him, and they stared at him, pleased.

"Now, remember to be charming," Sarah said.

"Charming?"

"Yes, compliment her and smile."

Maureen rested her hands on her hips. "Just for one night pretend to be someone else," she said, then winked.

The party was in full swing when Justin arrived. Holiday music floated through the air and mingled with the tinkling of glasses. The Rollinses had rented a small room in one of the hotels close to their house to host the party. He searched the crowd, wondering what his mystery woman would look like. Then his gaze fell on a familiar face. He froze, gripping the glass in his hand and hoping he wouldn't shatter it.

Chapter 4

Oliver walked up to Justin with a big grin. "Good—you're finally here."

"What's she doing here?"

"Who?"

He stared at Lora and motioned with his head. "Her."

"That's the woman my wife was talking about. *I just* found out that you both work in the same department. I know it might be awkward, but give it a chance."

"That's the woman who hates me."

"The stupid one?"

"She's not stupid." He turned. "It was a bad idea for me to come."

Oliver looked over at Lora then back at Justin, confused. "There must be a mistake."

Justin set his glass down and headed for the door.

"My dear, you're here," Anya called from behind him. "Where are you going? I'm ready to make introductions."

He reluctantly turned to her. "No, you don't want to do that."

She took his hand in an iron hold. "You're just shy. She won't bite."

He was stronger than her. He could lift her up and run if he wanted to, but he didn't want to cause a scene. "Don't do this," he said in a low desperate voice. "You don't understand. Let me explain."

"No need to. I know that other woman who hurt you made you shy of risking your heart again, but you can trust me. She's interested in science just like you."

"Anya," her husband said. "I think—"

"Stay out of it, Oliver. I know what I'm doing."

Oliver shrugged, sending Justin a helpless look as Anya led him away. As he got closer, Justin scrambled to think of what he could say. Then he noticed how her dress clung to her backside, and he again found himself thinking of her naked.

"Lora? This is Justin."

Lora spun around with a warm smile that immediately fell when she saw him. She stared at him in disbelief.

"Can I get you a drink?" he said, eager for a reason to leave.

"Isn't he such a gentleman?" Anya said. "I'll get drinks so you two can get to know each other."

"We already know each other," Justin said. "We work together."

"Oh, good. Office romances can be so much fun.

Then you don't need drinks. You must work up a thirst first. You should dance."

"I don't dance," Justin said.

"You can learn."

"I'd prefer to just talk."

"You can talk later. A dance tells you everything— like how well you move together," Anya insisted.

"Fine."

"What?" Lora sputtered.

He grabbed Lora's wrist and led her to the dance floor. "It's one dance. And the music's fast so we might as well get it over with."

The moment they reached the dance floor the music became slow. He glanced over at Anya and saw her giving him a thumbs-up.

"Just kill me now."

"What did you say?" Lora asked.

He pulled her into a dancer's embrace. "For just five minutes, pretend I'm someone else."

Lora could hardly breathe. This was all wrong. Anya must've gotten him confused with someone else. This was the kind, generous man she was describing? The man she knew had a spoiled niece and an arrogant manner. And why did he have to look so good and smell so wonderful? Without her anger, she had no shield against him. This close, she couldn't help but notice how solidly built he was, and her traitorous body enjoyed how it moved against him. And he moved well. How could a man who was so cold make her feel so hot? She briefly shut her eyes; she didn't want to think about it.

"At least there's no mistletoe," he said.

His deep silky voice was close to her ear, sending shivers of awareness through her. She could only nod her head, not trusting herself to speak.

"You look beautiful."

Her head snapped up. She stared at him, ready to hide behind anger. "Is that supposed to be a joke?"

He blinked. "No."

"My hair looks as if I've been electrocuted, I have a run in my stockings, my eyeliner would look better on a raccoon, and my blush is too red. You can thank my sister, Belinda, for this. Fortunately, I don't have to impress you."

"Your face is fine. Your eyeliner is too dark because it's the wrong shade. I can stop the run in your stocking if you have some nail polish with you, or better yet, you can take them off and put them in the freezer for a few minutes. As for the blush, it just needs to be softened."

Lora looked at him openmouthed.

He gently pulled her chin up with a finger and shrugged. "What? You think having one sister is bad, try being the youngest of three. Two of them ambushed me before I got here."

Lora smiled at the image of anyone having that kind of power of him. "Ambushed?"

"Yes, they went through my clothes, right down to my underwear. They said that 'answering the question right' was important."

"The question?"

"Boxers or briefs. They said women liked to know."

Lora bit her lip to stop herself from asking, although she *was* suddenly curious. He'd look good in both. She groaned. She didn't want to think about him wearing only his underwear, but it was too late.

"Is something wrong? Am I holding you too tightly or something?"

"No. Why?"

"You groaned."

"It's nothing," she said hoping the song would end soon. "Why didn't you stop them?"

"Blackmail."

"Blackmail?"

"Yes, they have compromising pictures of me that could destroy my reputation."

"How?"

"Let's just say that before I was born they liked to dress up their dolls and our dog Rachael."

Lora couldn't help a chuckle. "And then they turned on you?"

"Yes. They accepted me as a little sister."

Lora laughed. "You're making this up."

"No, I wish I were. I was wearing lipstick and bows until I was three."

"Didn't your parents say anything?"

"My parents are very lenient."

"They have pictures?"

"And a video."

"I'd give anything to see it."

His voice deepened. "Really?"

She swallowed and looked away. "You're right—you had it worse than me. My sister only smothers me because she thinks she's being protective." Belinda had always been her greatest ally against a strict, emotionally distant father who rarely found anything in Lora he liked. Their father had grown up in dire circumstances as the youngest of eleven children. Her grandfather had taken an instant dislike to him. He was convinced that his mother had been unfaithful and the child wasn't really his. Not only was his father distant, but he was also a cruel man. Both her father and her grandmother suffered great physical abuse at the hand of her grandfather. Now, for some reason, her father resented her more than Belinda. Before Lora knew it, she was telling Justin about Belinda and their childhood.

"She can turn any simple thing into an expedition. Just last weekend I had to go shopping with her. Thankfully I bumped into Warren…uh, Dr. Rappaport."

She felt him stiffen. "Be careful of him."

"Why?"

"Because he's interested in you."

"A woman can enjoy a man's interest."

"You can have mine."

Lora paused. Had she heard him correctly? Was he hitting on her? "But you're different."

"How so? I'm just like any other man."

Yes, he was definitely flirting with her. Wow—the book was working, and she still had two more chapters to go. But Silver? Dr. Silver was interested in her? And he was wrong. He wasn't like any man she'd ever met before. Lora made a noncommittal sound.

"You can trust me."

"And of course I should just take your word for it."

"Yes, I'm an honest guy."

"I know why Dr. Rappaport doesn't like you. Why don't you like him?"

"It's a long boring story. Just watch your step."

"Duly noted."

"And if he asks you out, say no."

"Too late. He's already asked me, and I said yes with capital letters."

"When?"

"I can't believe we're having this conversation. What I do in my private life is none of your business," Lora said, feeling conflicted and giddy at the same time. Was this really happening? Why was she really discussing her personal life with, of all people, Silver?

"I know. That's the problem."

"Problem?"

"Yes, I want to be part of your private life." His voice dropped, and his gaze lowered to her lips. "The more intimate, the better."

Lora licked her lips and swallowed, both alarmed and aroused. Was he truly interested in her? Worse, was she becoming interested in him? "I think you're more dangerous than he is."

His gaze met hers. "Don't make that mistake."

Lora stopped dancing. What was she doing? If she wasn't careful she'd start to like him. How could that be possible? He felt too good, too comfortable. His voice was hypnotizing her. She found herself straining to hear it, liking how his breath brushed against her cheek. She drew away. "I have to go."

She slipped out of his grasp, grabbed her purse then raced out the door, not caring that she was leaving her coat behind. The cold air would do her good.

* * *

Minutes later Anya found Justin sitting alone at the bar. "Where is she?"

"She left."

"What happened?"

"I don't know."

"And you didn't go after her?"

"I think it was better for both of us," he said. The longer he'd held her in his arms the more he'd enjoyed it. She'd moved in perfect harmony with him—how could he not be attracted to someone who fit him so well? To everyone there, they probably looked like a practiced dance team in synchrony with each other.

Anya frowned. "Never mind. She still has a lot to get over. I think too much happiness scares her. We'll give her time."

He raised his brows. "We will?"

"Yes. She likes you. I could tell by the way she was looking at you."

"Are you sure you were looking at the right woman?"

"Oh, yes. Oliver explained to me what you think, but you're wrong. She doesn't hate you."

"We have a past."

"That you both need to get over. I've never seen a better pair."

Justin shoved his hands in his pockets. He didn't want to sound like an eager schoolboy with a crush, but he couldn't help being curious. "So you really think she likes me?"

"I do. She's afraid to show it. "Anya smiled. "You like her, too?"

"I do."

She clapped her hands. "I already hear wedding bells."

"It's a bit early for that," he said but he took a long swallow of his drink to keep from whistling. She liked him. This was good. Before leaving, he grabbed her coat; he would make sure to put it in her office on Monday.

This wasn't good. Lora went home ready to strip down to nothing and stand in front of the freezer. She needed a cold shower to snap her back to her senses. Justin Silver could *not* be an option. She had to forget about him, about his hands and those lashes and that voice. It didn't matter that he could make her laugh or that he'd said she looked beautiful. He was just being polite. Unfortunately, that hadn't stop her from feeling good. No, terrific.

Lora marched into her apartment and then paced her living room. She had to forget about tonight. She had to replace it with something else. She needed to do something wild and reckless. She grabbed the book *30 Days to Romance,* flipped through the pages to Chapter 6 and began to read:

If you want things to change in your life, you can't do the things you've always been doing. You have to move past your comfort zone. Do something you wouldn't normally do. Here are some suggestions:

Lora scrolled her finger down the list then stopped at one suggestion that made her hair rise on the back of her neck. That was it. This was something she'd never usually do, but it would make for a memorable evening. Now all she needed was a man. She searched for Warren's phone number. He was the perfect distraction—easy to talk to and charming. And she knew he'd be game for a little fun. She had to do something to forget about Justin.

She took a long bath, lathered her body with an almond-milk lotion, then slipped into a new sexy nightdress she had bought for herself after reading Chapter 3: Self Love. She got into bed, then dialed.

"Hello?" a male voice answered, huskier than she expected.

Lora gripped the phone, ready to hang up. Just his voice made her forget herself.

"Hello?" he repeated.

"I know it's late," she said in a breathless rush before she lost courage, "but I couldn't stop thinking about you."

"Me, too," he said, and she heard the smile in his voice.

"Where are you right now?"

"In my living room."

Lora squeezed her eyes shut. It was now or never. "Well, I'm in bed wearing a red silk robe."

"Is it short or long?"

"Long. It feels really good against my skin. Don't you wish you could touch it?"

"I'd prefer to touch you."

She licked her lips. "Where do you want to touch me?"

"How much time do I have?"

"All the time you want."

"What I want to know is what's under the robe."

"Just me."

"I didn't think the night could get any better and now it just did."

"You sound even sexier on the phone. Almost not like yourself."

"Is that good or bad?"

"It's wonderful."

"Do you feel me taking your robe off?"

"How are you doing it?"

"I'm slowly untying your belt, my fingers brushing against your stomach. Do you feel that?"

"Yes."

"And now I'm sliding your robe back from your shoulders and ever so gently slipping it down the length of you."

Lora squirmed in bed, her body getting hot and wet. She listened to his voice describing how he would touch her breasts and thighs, kissing her in her most sacred places, and she felt every action as if he was in bed beside her, urging her to touch herself in that special place of ecstasy. She moaned.

"You like that?"

"Oh, yes."

"Now I'll—"

"Oh, no, you're not going to be the only one having fun."

"I thought you were."

"I am. But now I'm going to have some more." She pushed the covers aside. "Now it's your turn. I'm unbuttoning your shirt."

"You don't have to. I'm just wearing a T-shirt."

"Even better. I'm sliding it over your head. Now do I have to unzip or unbutton your trousers?"

"They're jeans and you can unzip them."

"Which is exactly what I'm doing now. Am I going to find boxers or briefs?"

"Boxers."

"Good. I'm sliding my hand up one of the legs."

"You're not going to take them off?"

"Not yet, right now I'm going to do a bit of search and discover. Oh, yes, I like what I feel. Do you like how I'm touching you?"

"Hmm."

"You feel so good and hard." She imagined she could feel his manhood, describing to him what she was doing with her hands.

"Are you still there?"

"I wouldn't want to be anywhere else."

"Wasn't this amazing? I've never done something like this before. I wasn't sure how you'd feel about it."

"You can call me anytime."

Lora laughed at his eagerness. "I'm in heaven."

"You're lucky, I'm not allowed to go there."

"Because you've been a bad boy?"

"Very bad."

"Good. Stay that way," she said.

Lora dressed with extra care that Monday morning. The book was working, and she still had one more chapter left. She'd definitely made progress with Warren and had taken their relationship to a new level. When she saw him in the hall between labs she winked.

He walked up to her and grinned. "Someone's in a good mood."

"I had a great weekend."

"Really? What did you do?"

She playfully hit him in the stomach.

"Don't act as if you don't know why."

"I don't."

She glanced around then lowered her voice. "The phone call."

"What phone call?"

"From Saturday night."

"I didn't get a phone call."

Lora took out her phone. "But I called you. Isn't this your number?"

"It looks right. But I never remember because I don't call myself. Oh, wait." He swore.

"What?"

"I mixed up three numbers."

Lora's heart started to race. "You gave me the wrong number?"

"It was a mistake."

"How could you do this to me?"

"Do what?"

She couldn't tell him. She couldn't tell anyone. She wanted to strangle him and then find a hole to bury herself. "Forget it."

Oh, God, she'd called some stranger and had phone sex. Okay, fine. He didn't know who she was. Even if he did call, she could block him. She would survive this.

Strange how he'd sounded so familiar. She *knew* that voice. That beautiful, deep, sexy voice. She glanced up and saw Justin talking to Carla. She couldn't have called him. What were the odds? No. No. No. It was some stranger. Justin would have called her a nut and hung up. He wouldn't have touched her like that or let her touch him. He glanced up and saw her staring. That's when he did something she'd never seen him do before. He smiled at her.

Chapter 5

Oh, no. Oh, no! What was she going to do? She watched him disappear into Carla's office.

"Silver looks pleased with himself," Warren said.

Lora made a noncommittal sound, her mind racing.

"You know why, right?"

She turned to him, startled. "Do you?" she said in a strangled voice. How could he know? Had Justin bragged about the phone call?

"Yes, he's been busy causing havoc. He transferred me from the project I was working on with Dr. Yung and refused Carla's funding request."

"What?"

"Yes, I bet he's telling her the news now."

Lora turned when she saw Carla's door open. She came out with Justin, wiping her eyes in a quick motion. She was not an expressive woman, and it tore at the very heart of Lora to see Justin make her friend so unhappy.

Lora shook her head. "I can't believe this."

Warren shoved his hands in his pockets and rocked on his heels. "Believe it. She's out in the cold. She'll have to scramble to restructure her team and function on the funding she has now."

Lora clenched her hands into fists. He'd already decided the fate of one friend's life. She wouldn't let him decide another's.

Justin walked into Oliver's office, pleased that his talk with Carla had gone well. He hadn't been sure how she would take the news, but she had been professional as always. He sat in front of Oliver's desk. "You wanted to speak to me?"

"Yes, a former colleague of mine, Dr. Patrick Ruthers, has a special research project in Minnesota. He's uncovered crucial samples that need to be analyzed."

"Samples?"

"Yes. He's a little eccentric but brilliant. He runs his own certified lab in the basement of his house, and he's dealt with the transplantation of blood-forming stem cells. He's discovered a unique set of samples taken from individuals living on two small islands in the Pacific, where sickle cell has been found to be endemic. They live long productive lives and suffer only a few crises throughout their lifetime."

"That's great," Justin said, intimately aware of the statistic that here in the United States, up until the past two decades, most people with sickle cell anemia only lived to their early thirties. He considered each birthday after thirty to be a miracle.

"Ruthers wants to keep this study quiet, so he's asked me to send him two skilled scientists who have knowledge in the area and who also are able to keep their mouths shut. Secrecy and discretion are of the utmost importance. He needs someone for next week, so it's a quick turnaround. I wanted your suggestions."

"Send Rice and me."

"You?"

"Yes."

Oliver frowned. "The winters there at this time of year are brutal. Let's send Rappaport, and…"

"He's far from discreet. He couldn't keep a secret if it were covered in concrete. Besides he's not one of our best."

"Then give me the name of someone else."

"I just did."

"Besides you."

"It's only a week. I can do this."

"And Rice is still…young. I saw your evaluation. You criticized some of her methods."

"But she's a solid scientist. She wouldn't be in the running for the fellowship if she wasn't. She can do this with my guidance."

"What about your tension with her?"

"We're professionals," Justin said with a smug grin. "Plus, that won't be a problem anymore."

Oliver's brows shot up. "Things have changed?"

His grin widened. "More than you know."

"You don't need to do this. It'll only be for a week and when she gets back will you—"

"I'll be fine. And she's committed to this disease like no one else."

"I thought you wanted to focus on winning the fellowship."

"This matters more."

Oliver sat back, reluctantly pleased. "You like her that much?"

"Yes."

"Okay. Pack your bags…you're going to Minnesota."

"Rice? I need to talk to you."

Lora looked up from her desk and glared at Justin. "I'm busy, Dr. Silver. Perhaps—"

"This won't take long." He turned and walked to his office.

Lora gritted her teeth and followed him, but she didn't sit. She folded her arms and waited. She hadn't had a chance to talk to Carla yet and was still planning her strategy.

He paced behind his desk, then stopped and looked at her. "I know that I should probably wait to tell you this, but I can't. I spoke to Dr. Rollins and got him to put us on a project together. We'll be spending a week in Minnesota, and we leave in two days. It's a great opportunity for us. We'll be analyzing a group of select samples, part of sickle cell anemia research being conducted in a private lab facility run by a close friend of Dr. Rollins. At first Rollins didn't want to use you because of your limited background and lack of more extensive experience in the area. I also had some misgivings, but I thought this was too good an opportunity for you to miss. So I convinced him that you would meet the standard."

"I can't go," Lora said in a flat tone. "Please find someone else. Is that all?" she asked, ready to leave.

Justin paused, surprised by her refusal. "Is there a schedule conflict? We'll be back before the holidays."

"That's not it."

"Then what is it?" he asked, stumbling over his words.

"I'm sorry you went through all this trouble, but I'm not interested."

"You're not interested? I don't understand."

"I'm sorry I haven't been clear. The truth is, I don't want to go with you."

Justin's gaze fell. "But the other night—"

"Was a mistake. I called you by accident."

His gaze flew up, but he remained silent.

"I got the numbers mixed up with Warren's," she continued, warming to her subject. "Do you honestly think I'd want to do something like that with you?" Her hands flew to her hips. "A man who takes gifts from little girls? Who gets guys kicked out of school? Who stops funding for talented researchers just because you have the power to?"

Justin rolled his eyes, and his mouth spread into a cynical smile. "Oh, I see that you've been talking to Rappaport again. I told you to be careful of him."

"Because you don't like him."

"Because he talks too much."

"Or because he's more popular than you?"

"Careful, Lora. I've warned you about jumping to conclusions."

"Did you or did you not buy a gift for your niece that he wanted for his sick cousin?"

"Yes."

"Did you get him kicked out of school?"

"Yes."

"Okay, and do you deny that you removed him from the project he was working on with Dr. Yung's team and refused Carla's request for extra funding?"

"I have nothing to deny. I don't regret the decisions I've had to make."

"And that's all that matters to you. You thought you could impress me like this? By highlighting how you overlooked my shortcoming for this opportunity and that my lack of experience wouldn't matter?"

"I wasn't trying to impress you—I was stating fact. Was I supposed to flatter you with pretty words that are untrue? I thought you were above that."

"The most offensive part is how you've come to me with this project, acting as if I should be grateful. You stand there expecting me to be impressed by your degrees and accomplishments as you tell me what you've decided for me. Dr. Silver, you may have succeeded as a scientist, but you've failed as a man. I'd rather rot in a dungeon than spend five minutes doing fascinating research with you—"

Justin held up his hand. "Okay, you've made yourself clear. I'm sorry I bothered you."

She turned, then halted when she saw Dr. Rollins staring at her. She'd forgotten that she'd left the office door open.

"I don't believe this. Rice, what is wrong with you?"

She swallowed. "Dr. Rollins, I—"

He looked past her to Justin, who was coming out from behind his desk. "I knew I shouldn't have listened to you," Dr. Rollins said, not looking at Lora.

Justin gestured to a seat. "Come in. I can explain."

"I'm sure you can. You're always covering for bad behavior, but not this time." Oliver glared at Lora. "I had my doubts about you, but this is worse than I thought. To see you so disrespectful to your director is atrocious. To say such awful things when you have no idea what this man has done. What he has gone through to get here. Do you think because you've gotten here with special recommendations that you're above everyone else?"

"Oliver, enough," Justin said. "It's okay."

"Okay?" Oliver said, shooting Lora a look of disgust. "If this is how she behaves, then your evaluation was much kinder than it should have been."

Carla suddenly appeared. "I'm sure it's all a misunderstanding, Dr. Rollins," she said, taking Lora's arm in a firm grip. "Excuse us." She dragged Lora to her office.

Once in her office, Carla shut the door and pointed to a seat. "Sit down."

"I don't want—"

Carla narrowed her eyes. "I don't care."

Lora sat.

"What has gotten into you lately?"

"What do you mean?"

"How can you speak to Dr. Silver that way?"

"I was telling him how I felt."

"By shouting at him like a fishwife?"

"I wasn't shouting."

"You didn't even have the decency to close the door. You could be heard down the hall. Warren was doubled over in laughter."

"He was?"

"I, unfortunately, didn't find it funny."

Lora sighed. "I guess I let my temper get the better of me. I'm sorry."

"What you did was outrageous. Silver deserves better from you."

Lora widened her eyes. "How can you defend him after what he did to you?"

"What did he do to me?"

"He refused your request for extra funding."

"So?"

Lora straightened. "He also got Warren thrown out of a program and then he *tells* me, doesn't even ask, *tells* me, that I'm going to work on a special project with him in Minnesota and—"

Carla shook her head. "That doesn't matter. What you did was incredibly reckless."

"Reckless?" Lora said. "First Dr. Rollins and now you? Doesn't anyone see my side or even Warren's side? Will we always need to bow down to Silver's dictate?"

"And just how solid is Warren's side of the story? What proof do you have to back it up?"

"Why would he lie?"

"What would any man lie? Have you forgotten how powerful Justin is? The respect he has in the field?

The contributions he's made? You just passed up a prime position, a great opportunity to delve into research close to your heart just because of something the man you have a crush on said?"

"You make it sound juvenile."

"Because that's how you behaved. If that's the kind of advice that book of yours is telling you, I want you to throw it away the second you get home."

"You're making an assumption that what Warren said isn't true. Dr. Silver admitted to everything," Lora said.

"Yes, and naturally you took the time to hear the full story before you jumped to your conclusion, correct?"

"Well, no, but—"

"That's what I thought. You overestimate your ability to assess situations, Lora. You always have. You have a quick mind, but it's both a strength and a weakness." Carla sat back. "I can't comment about what Warren's told you about the school program, but I can clarify the other two. First, Dr. Silver didn't cruelly remove Warren. He wasn't performing well and would have been fired if Silver hadn't stepped in. Dr. Yung had given him several warnings that his performance needed to improve or he would be out of a job. Silver actually created a new assignment with Dr. Yung so that wouldn't happen. Second, he cut funding for my current project because he wants me to head a major pain management research project working with Johns Hopkins University and George Washington University. This is a dream come true for me. Silver's sharp when it comes to seizing opportunities—that's how he's gotten this far."

"But he made you cry! I saw you standing outside of your office with him. He's known for making people cry."

"I was crying because I was happy. I know Silver can be tactless and distant, but did you even wonder why Rappaport has been so quick to confide all his troubles to you? He's hardly been here six months, yet he's made you his confidant. If you wanted to know what had happened, all you had to do was come and ask me."

"He confided in me because we both don't like Silver."

"And he used that knowledge to his advantage. Even if what Rappaport said was true, you still could have behaved with dignity. What references do you expect Silver to give you? If for no other reason than to keep your career on track you should apologize, even if it's halfhearted."

"I just thought—"

"Stop thinking and just listen. Right now you're blind, so I'll open your eyes. Silver likes you. That means new opportunities and contacts. But Rappaport just closed that door for you. You look bad to both Silver and Rollins because you're a wild card. And guess who's waiting to step up into your space?"

Lora felt her heart fall.

Carla continued. "Dr. Rollins heard your outburst. You keep wanting to blame Silver for halting your career, but now you can only blame yourself."

"What can I do?"

"I honestly don't know. I can try to talk to Silver for you, but Dr. Rollins did not look pleased. I think it's out of our hands."

"But I thought he was doing to you what he'd done to Suzette."

"What did he do?"

"He let her die."

"Stop being dramatic. That's not what happened. I was there, remember? I'd been working with Silver at the time. I was there when you shouted at him and when he came after you."

"I don't remember…"

"Exactly. You've made yourself forget what you need to remember if you really want to heal. You want to be angry at him. You want to blame him, but you need to stop. Close your eyes and remember that day. He came after you…"

Memories she'd buried came flooding back. Lora remembered pacing the waiting room floor, knowing she had to compose herself before seeing Suzette and Mrs. Gannotti again. She hated the feeling of helplessness that gripped her. She remembered seeing Carla standing by the vending machine—she'd been one of the white coats in Suzette's room. She'd barely noticed. Carla had given Lora a brief, compassionate smile that Lora ignored. All she saw was another white coat who was part of an institution that didn't care or understand how awful it felt to lose her friend. What would her life be like without Suzette?

"Stop being so selfish."

Lora had spun around, startled by the harsh, deep command. She'd glared up at Justin.

"What did you just say?"

"You're not helping your friend by making her feel that she's failing you. You're not doing her any favors by thinking of yourself instead of her."

"I'm not."

"Aren't you wondering about what you'll do without her? How you'll manage? Did you once think about how it must feel for her to be in that hospital bed, receiving few visitors? Not seeing people who you care about but who don't want to see you? You may not realize, but you see her as a disease. You see her as something broken that needs to be fixed. And you're scared by how she is now. If you truly love her, give her the gift of letting her go."

His words had pierced her heart. "You have no right to tell me how to feel."

"No, I don't. But I can say this. You want me to regret the decisions I've made, but I won't. You will. If she passes on with things left unsaid between the two of you or without you by her side, it will haunt you for the rest of your life. I know you don't like me, but that doesn't matter. Suzette is all that matters. Think about it. Arguing with me and hating the doctors or the nurses won't change anything. Be a friend," he'd said. Then he had turned and walked away.

That night Lora had gone back into Suzette's hospital room and knew she didn't want her friend to feel anything but love. "Thank you for being the best friend in the world. You've made my life so much brighter."

Suzette didn't speak then, but Lora had seen her

eyes light up for a moment. A few minutes later, she was gone.

As Lora opened her eyes in Carla's office she was forced to admit that Justin had given her that moment. She'd been so focused on fighting the disease that she'd forgotten what her friend needed—her presence. If she'd spent more time arguing with the doctors, she would not have been at Suzette's side when she died. Yes, he'd given her that, but she'd made herself forget because she wanted to be angry—at him. His presence was always forcing her to face a truth she didn't want to see. She had lost her dearest friend and needed someone, anyone to blame.

Lora realized, for the first time, that he was the one man who could make her stop feeling numb. He had reawakened emotion in her: rage, despair, even attraction. She had to admit that he'd been right. There was nothing they could have done. That was what angered her—the truth he forced her to see. He'd taken away her hope, but hope had already gone.

Carla sighed. "You know, one day you're going to have to shout at your father instead of at every man who reminds you of him."

Lora jumped to her feet. She didn't want to talk about her father or her misjudgment. "Thank you," she said, then rushed out of Carla's office.

Yes, she had been blind, rash and foolish. She needed to think. There had to be something she could do to fix things.

Chapter 6

"She must be suspended immediately," Oliver said to Justin. "I'll have Carla go with you to Minnesota."

Justin sat behind his desk, straightening his pens. "It's okay."

"Stop saying that. It's *not* okay. Is this how she behaves? This is the woman you said was discreet?"

"You caught her at a bad time. She's—"

"Are you thinking with the right organ? I can't have someone like that represent us."

Justin took a long drink from his thermos, wishing he had something stronger to drink than just water. Lora's words were more painful than any attack he'd ever experienced, but he couldn't let his friend know that. Lora's career was on the line, and he didn't want Rappaport to get away with ruining it.

"Oliver, I want you to trust me. I haven't steered you wrong before. I will not let you and Dr. Ruthers down. In two days, Rice and I will leave for Minnesota and get the job done." He grabbed an aspirin, popped it in his mouth, then drank more water.

"Are you all right?"

"It's just a headache."

"I want to stop you from doing this, but...fine. I'll let you have your way. Another outburst like that, though, and she's gone."

"Agreed."

Oliver nodded, then left. Justin resisted resting his head on the desk. He'd have plenty of time to rest when he got home that evening, but for now, he had an entire day to get through. He inwardly groaned when someone knocked on his door.

"Come in," he said, feeling as if saying those two words had taken what remaining energy he had left.

Warren strolled in and took a seat. "Dr. Rice didn't sound very happy. What was that all about?"

"I'm sure you know."

"Thanks for putting in a good word for me with Dr. Yung."

"As if I had a choice. You're still spreading your lies like fertilizer."

Warren shrugged. "And watching things grow."

"Stay away from Lora."

"I don't need her anymore. And if I do, there's nothing you can do about it. The ladies have always liked me more than they like you."

"I'm not going to cover for you again."

"Does she know about you? Or is that still your big secret?"

Justin lowered his voice. "Don't threaten me."

Warren leaned against the desk, unfazed. "I saw one of your crises, remember? I could describe it to her in great detail. Would you like that?" He came around the desk. "You'll be lucky if you make it to your next birthday. And I need this job. You got in my way once before, but I've learned from my mistakes. This is just a taste of what I can do. So stay out of my way." He walked to the door, then looked over his shoulder. "Just a little friendly advice," he said as he left.

Justin turned to the window. Maybe he'd lost his touch. He used to have his life in order, but now the woman he liked truly despised him and he had to cover for a man he hated. He stared at the holiday decorations on the buildings outside, and for the first time in his life he felt empty.

This was war. Lora approached Warren just as he was getting into his car. She grabbed his car door before he could close it.

"You set me up," she said.

"Why would I do that?"

"You didn't make a mistake. You didn't switch phone numbers around. I checked. You gave me the wrong number on purpose. When you texted me it was from a blocked number. That should have been my first warning."

"It was supposed to be a joke. A harmless prank. I thought it would be a great kick to Silver's ego to find out that you were calling me instead of him. I thought you'd say something like 'Hello, Warren' and then he'd hang up."

"That didn't happen."

He stepped out of his car and rested against it. "What did?"

She folded her arms; she'd never tell him. "*And* you lied."

"No, I didn't."

"You said he refused Carla's funding and removed you from a project."

"And he did."

"But that's not the whole story."

"So?" He flashed a charming grin. "I don't want you to be angry with me. Let me make it up to you. Are we still on for our date Saturday?"

"Absolutely not."

He moved in close and brushed the back of his hand against her cheek.

Lora pushed his hand away and stepped back. "Don't you ever touch me again."

"I thought you liked me."

"I did."

He shook his head. "Women can be so fickle. Don't tell me you're getting it on with Silver."

"I'm not getting it on with anyone," she said.

"That's not a surprise, but I can change that. I know you want me. I can tell. I noticed the first moment we met."

"Well, let's just say, I can see more clearly now. And do you want to know what I see?"

"What?" he asked, clearly uninterested.

"You're jealous of Silver. You resent everything that he has because you want it for yourself. I didn't see that before."

Warren's eyes grew hard. "I'm not jealous."

"You're so far beneath him you can hardly see the daylight."

He shrugged and got back into his car. "You can't prove anything, and Silver can't touch me. So why don't you go home and cool off so that you can pray?"

"Pray?"

"Yes, pray that you'll still have a job to come back to." He slammed the car door shut, then drove away.

That night Lora sat in her apartment feeling like the loneliest woman in the world. How could she have been so wrong about Warren? He'd seemed so sincere. But Carla was right—he'd been too eager to share all his grievances about Justin with her and she'd eaten it up. She'd been unprofessional, and even worse, she'd been as unfair and callous as she'd once accused Justin of being. She'd given one man too much credit and the other too little. She was undisciplined and did jump to conclusions. How could Justin have ever liked her? What had he seen, and why hadn't she noticed? It didn't matter now. He probably didn't want anything to do with her anymore and she didn't blame him. She didn't like herself today, either.

Lora turned on the radio and a holiday song came through the speakers. She immediately switched it off. She'd donate the book that had caused all this. No, she'd burn it. Carla was right—she hadn't been herself, and she didn't like who she'd become after Suzette's death. It would be another lonely holiday, except this time she'd be without a job. She wouldn't wait to be suspended; she'd leave gracefully. She sat down at her kitchen table, powered up her laptop and typed a letter of resignation. After she'd hit the Send button she called her sister.

"I really messed up," she said.

"What happened?"

She told her about Warren, Justin and Dr. Rollins.

"Warren? Why does that name sound familiar?"

"Because he's the guy you met at the mall."

Belinda swore. "I knew I shouldn't have left you alone with him."

"It's more my fault than his. I just resigned. I know Dad's going to enjoy this. He's always thought I was a loser."

"He doesn't have to know. And you'll get a new job. Don't worry—everything will work out."

They talked for a few more minutes, and Lora hung up, wishing she could believe her sister.

Belinda fumed. She'd never heard her sister sound so defeated. She remembered Lora recovering from the death of Suzette, and now her voice was eerily close to her helplessness then. That Warren guy had really hurt her. Belinda wrung her hands, her mind racing. What could she do? Nobody messed with her little sister. She would make sure that Warren Rappaport paid.

You're accomplished as a scientist, but you've failed as a man. Justin pushed his dinner around on his plate as Lora's words echoed in his mind. She'd looked at him as if he was some awful bacteria she'd found growing in a petri dish. And the phone call had been a mistake—she didn't want him, she'd wanted Rappaport. Justin gripped his fork, remembering Rappaport's visit to his office and his smug grin. The slimy eel had won again. If only he didn't know about Justin's secret, then he could fight him. But Rappaport never fought fair. Now the bastard had Lora believing every word he said.

"Justin?"

He glanced up at his youngest sister, Ann. She'd invited him for dinner, just as she did once a month. He looked at her worried face and then noticed that no one else was around the table. The dishes had been cleared.

He forced a smile. "Sorry. I got lost in thought. Let me help you in the kitchen."

"You've hardly eaten anything."

"What I ate was delicious, as always."

"You can't afford to skip meals."

"I'm not." He carried the dishes to the sink.

Ann followed him. "What's wrong?"

"Nothing."

"Something's bothering you. I can tell."

"Well, for work I have to travel soon, but I'll be back in time for Christmas."

"Good. It wouldn't be the same without you. You know Monique and Jayla love seeing you."

"Yes."

"They keep asking when they'll get a new aunty."

"No, they don't."

"You're right. I'm the one who wants to know."

Justin helped load the dishwasher. "You know how I feel."

"You can't let it stop you from having a full life. Maureen and Sarah told me you were meeting a woman at a party. How did it go?"

"Great," he lied.

She pounced. "Really? What is she like? When can I meet her?"

"But it didn't work out. She's interested in someone else."

"Let me meet her."

"Forget it. It wasn't meant to be."

"You know that day you came home from school sad because none of the kids would play with you after you'd been released from the hospital?"

"Yes."

"Well, you have that exact expression now. You look like that lonely little boy on the playground, and it breaks my heart. Tell me what's going on."

He turned on the dishwasher, then kissed her cheek. "I'm fine. I'm a man now—not a little boy you have to worry about."

Later that night, as Justin drove home from his sister's place, he thought of her words. He didn't want to be lonely anymore. He wouldn't surrender and let Warren win. He didn't usually explain himself, but he'd tell Lora the truth. He'd make her listen. He'd make her learn to trust him, eventually. They were a good team, even if she didn't see it yet. He'd get Lora to see the real him. He'd make her see him as a man. The perfect man for her.

Chapter 7

Carla sat in her favorite café wondering what she could do to help her friend. She knew that approaching Justin now wouldn't be a good idea. Perhaps it would be best to leave them both to sort it out. Carla sipped her coffee, then glanced over at a young man trying to calm a screaming infant. If he didn't succeed soon the other customers might have him thrown out. One went over to a cashier and pointed to the young man. Carla felt sorry for the new father. She knew how it felt to not belong.

She recalled signing up for an aerobics class and discovering that she was not only the oldest member in the group, but also the most uncoordinated. She had as much elegance as a giraffe on roller skates. The instructor had coolly suggested that she try something "less strenuous." She stood up and dashed over to the father before the manager was called.

"Give her to me," she demanded.

The young man looked up at her, startled, then handed her the baby. Carla held the baby and soon the crying stopped.

"Wow, that was amazing," the man said. "I've never met a baby whisperer before."

Carla laughed. "No, I just have lots of practice. I babysat through high school and college. There were lots of new mothers in my neighborhood." And she'd really needed the money, but she didn't mention that.

She looked at the man closely and realized he wasn't as young as she'd first assumed. He was probably in his early to mid thirties. He had a nice open face and a five-o'clock shadow that made him look vulnerable rather than gruff. But what she found most interesting was the faint shimmer of glitter on his face.

"Can I buy you a coffee?" he asked. "Please," he added when she started to refuse. He stood up. "What can I get you?"

"I have my purse and things at that table."

"I'll get them for you. Just tell me what I can get you."

She gave him her order, then sat at his table. She glanced down and saw several textbooks and loose papers strewn all over the area next to his laptop.

The man returned to the table and set down her drink.

"Looks like you're trying to accomplish a lot," she said.

"Yes, I'm all done with my coursework except for my dissertation."

"Good for you. Is your wife a student, too?"

"No. I don't have a wife."

"Oh, sorry. I must seem so old-fashioned to you. I mean your girlfriend."

"I don't have a girlfriend, either."

"Boyfriend?"

He grinned. "No."

"Oh."

"It's just Ariel and me."

"And you are?"

"I'm Griffin Holt. And you are…?"

"Carla Petton."

"I know a lot of people think I'm trying to do too much, but 'I've got great ambition to die of exhaustion rather than boredom.'"

"Thomas Carlyle?"

"Exactly. I guess I need to quote more obscure figures so that I can impress women like you with my wit."

She laughed. "I'm already impressed. I have one question."

"Okay, what is it?"

"What's the story behind the glitter on your face?"

He wiped his cheek. "Really? Where?"

"Near your chin."

He gave it a brush. "Gone?"

"No."

He turned his face to her. "Wipe it off for me."

She used her thumb to swipe it off. "What have you been doing?"

"Helping the university's theater team with the stage set for *A Christmas Carol*."

"Sounds exciting. I used to do some acting in my younger days."

"So not very long ago?"

"A flatterer."

"I mean every word."

Carla felt her face grow warm. She glanced down at Ariel, who was now fast asleep. She was a beautiful baby. Her skin was the color of dark, dark chocolate, with silky, pitch-black eyebrows and lashes. She was a little on the chubby side, with a short fluffy afro framing her perfectly round face, with pink cupid lips that looked almost unreal, like they had been pasted on by a sculptor. "I guess I should—"

"What do you do?" he asked quickly, as if he didn't want her to leave.

"I'm a scientist."

"Tell me about it."

So she told him about Ventico Labs and about her vision for the new research she would be heading. He listened like few people did and asked interesting questions. Soon they were chatting like old friends. Then it was his turn. They talked for another forty-five minutes about his dissertation and plans for the future, and when she finally glanced at her watch Carla was shocked by the time. "I'd better dash."

"I should, too." He gathered up his things.

Carla grabbed Ariel's coat and put it on her. She could see that it was new and an expensive label, unlike the coat he wore, which was fraying at the edges. It was clear his priority right now was his daughter's welfare. She wanted to know more about him, including why he was a single father. She set Ariel in the stroller, but the baby squirmed and scrunched up her face, ready to cry again. "No, don't do that," Carla said, putting a pacifier in her trembling mouth. Ariel looked at her and calmed. Carla smiled at her then straightened and looked up. She saw Griffin staring, and Carla released a nervous laugh. "I'm sorry. I was taking liberties, wasn't I?"

"You were great. You're so calm and gentle with her. It's nice to see."

Carla didn't know what to say so she just nodded and grabbed her coat. He rushed around the table and helped her put her it on, his fingers brushing her neck.

"Would you like to go?" he asked. "To the play, I mean."

"I don't know."

"I could get you tickets if you want. One for you and Mr. Petton."

"There isn't a Mr. Petton."

"A significant other?"

"No."

He grinned. "Good, that's what I hoped you'd say. What's your number?"

Lora was under her bed covers when the phone rang. She swallowed when she recognized the number. It was Justin. She'd been a coward and not spoken to anyone at the office since emailing her resignation. Would she be fired over the phone? No, she couldn't get fired after she'd already resigned.

"Hello?"

"It's Silver. Don't hang up—just hear me out. You asked me once to tell you about Warren. I met him more than ten years ago when we both attended a scientific symposium in Hawaii. We were on a panel featuring young upcoming scientists, and we were required to make a ten-minute presentation. When it came time for Rappaport's presentation, several of the attendees caused a scene, claiming he had stolen their thesis idea and presented it as his own. They were hastily removed, but I decided to look into the allegations, and although it could not be proven beyond a reasonable doubt, I supported their accusations.

"So I sent a note to the magazine that had initially published his work, and they sent a letter to Rappaport informing him that they would put a small retraction in the upcoming issue, stating they were not liable for any omission of truth or subsequent revelations regarding the article he had written.

"Although I had hoped I would remain anonymous, somehow Rappaport found out that I was the so-called whistleblower. He eventually ended up leaving the university, where he was doing his graduate work. And regarding that toy, the Digital Dilly, he may have a sick cousin, but I doubt he'd give anything to her. He's estranged from every family member he has. Besides, I'm sure he didn't mention that he was able to get a rain check and his Digital Dilly will arrive by Christmas Eve. Anyway, that's all I can say about him, and I hope we can now consider this chapter closed. So are you packed yet?"

"Packed?" Lora repeated. "Didn't you get my letter?"

"Amazing what the delete button can do. Now, answer my question."

"Am I packed?"

"Yes, for tomorrow's flight. I know you don't want to go, but we couldn't get a replacement at such a short notice. I'll meet you at the airport. I sent you an email with all the information. Don't be late."

Lora stared at the phone, then hung up. If Justin was to be believed, Warren was even worse than she'd imagined. One thing was for certain, as much as she didn't want to, she was going to have to face Justin again.

Chapter 8

Minnesota

The taxi driver had been talking almost nonstop since
picking them up at the airport. Lora found him a comforting contrast to the man sitting beside her. She and
Justin had barely spoken since meeting at the airport
back in Baltimore. They hadn't been assigned seats
close together on the plane, and except for a few terse
words, they might as well have been complete strangers. She knew it was her fault. The picture she'd painted
of him had been completely wrong and now she had
to try to see him in a new light. She had to see him as
a man. A man who could be distant but considerate.
A man who didn't suffer fools gladly but still offered
a second chance. He'd given her one. She was sure he
could have gotten a replacement on short notice be-

cause there were plenty of other researchers in the lab who would have jumped at an opportunity like this. She owed him an apology—but more than that, she wanted this project to work.

She pulled out her cell phone and texted him.

You were right.

She surreptitiously watched him pull his cell phone out of his jacket and glance down. She couldn't read his face. Would he accept her apology?

She looked down at her phone when a reply popped up.

About what?

Warren. He's a creep.

I told u so.

I already feel like a worm. U don't have to step on me.

I'm not. I'm agreeing with u.

Why didn't u stop me? Why didn't u tell me how wrong I was?

Would u have listened?

Lora sighed, feeling ashamed.

Probably not.

I can't stop you from thinking the worst about me, but I'm not a bad guy.

I know. I shouldn't have jumped to conclusions. I've learned my lesson.

Good.

And I'm sorry.

How sorry?

She turned to him, but his profile was like granite. Was he being serious?

Is there a scale?

Yes.

If I could turn back time and erase it from memory, I would.

Everything? Even the phone call?

Her face burned. She was too startled to reply. Lora reread the text to make sure it was real. What could she say? She bit her lip, not daring to look at him.

"We're here," the driver announced.

Lora yanked her head up and lost her grip on her phone, which fell to the floorboard. She bent down to grab it, but it slid under the front seat.

"Want me to help you?" Justin said.

"No, I'm fine." She finally wrapped her hand around her phone's smooth surface. She straightened, then looked up and stared through the windshield. She saw an imposing structure. It looked abandoned.

"Are you sure this is the right place?" she asked, opening the taxi door. She looked around. It seemed so empty. She turned and saw Justin removing their bags from the trunk. "Something doesn't feel right."

"Jumping to conclusions again?"

"No, but—"

"This is the location I was given." He paid the taxi driver, then walked up to the front door. "They're expecting us. It's all been arranged." He knocked, then rang the doorbell. No answer.

He frowned. "That's odd. They knew we were coming."

Lora hugged herself, but it was a flimsy shield against the biting cold. Justin's phone rang. He answered and she saw his face change. "Oliver….What do you mean you've been trying to reach me? Yes, we're here. We just arrived….What? Why didn't anyone tell us this before? Of course I'm angry. The taxi's gone and we can't get inside. Okay, but…" He nodded. "I understand that but what are we supposed to do in the meantime?" He listened, then sighed. "Okay." He disconnected.

Lora cringed. "It's bad, isn't it?"

"Yes, the project's been cancelled. Yesterday, a lab technician mishandled the remaining samples and ruined them. So the lab's been shut down for the holidays. Dr. Ruthers told the technician to make sure to get the information to Dr. Rollins, but she didn't send the email until early this morning. Dr. Ruthers has already gone on vacation to Bermuda."

Lora rubbed her hands together and bounced up and down, trying to keep warm. "Well, what are we supposed to do?"

"Wait. Oliver said he'll get back to me in a second with the security code so that we can enter the building. Dr. Ruthers said we should make ourselves comfortable until we can fly back home."

"I hope it's soon. I'm freezing."

Justin took off his scarf and wrapped it around her.

"But—"

"Just be quiet."

"I don't want you to be cold."

Justin lifted his collar. "I'll be fine. Besides, I'm cold-blooded, remember?"

Lora moved closer, untied part of his scarf and wrapped it around him. "It's long enough to share, so don't argue. I can't stand here having you look as cold as I feel." The scarf brought them closer than she'd expected, but it felt oddly comforting being near him.

His cell phone rang.

"I'll get that," she said before he could protest. She reached inside his coat and grabbed his phone. "Dr. Rollins?"

"Rice? Where's Silver?"

"He's busy. Do you have the code to enter the building?"

"Yes." He gave her the combination.

"Thanks, Dr. Rollins, and I apologize for my unprofessional behavior the other day. It was way out of order and will never happen again."

"Good, then I need you to do me a favor without asking questions. Make sure you both get inside and warm up as fast as possible and drink plenty of liquids."

"Will do." She disconnected the cell phone, then entered the code in the keypad near the door. The alarm shut off, and they entered. The place was freezing. Lora searched for the thermostat, raised it, then looked around. For a moment, Lora thought they had entered a medieval castle. Stacks of books and piles of papers were everywhere. In the entryway off to the side rose a spiral staircase that appeared to lead up to a small loft above. Then there was the main staircase leading to the second floor. The house had an eerie feeling because of the dark wood paneling that lined the hallway and each of the rooms. What she assumed was the family room was filled with an array of stuffed wild game, including a snowy white owl and a red fox. "Wow, I guess he must enjoy hunting," Lora said.

Justin came into the room. "Oliver told me that he's a little eccentric. Actually, I think these animals may have been his pets. Look, they have names. He must have had them stuffed after they died."

They wandered around some more and found a small room off the kitchen that had a TV and a radio. "At least we will be able to keep ourselves entertained," Justin said.

Since they weren't going to be conducting any experiments, they did not venture to the basement, the location of Dr. Ruther's private lab. Plus a large sign reading "DO NOT ENTER" was posted on the door to the basement, *and* it was padlocked.

Lora looked at Justin as he set their bags in the

small living area. He looked a bit pale. She knew it best not to ask if he was okay because he'd lie and say he was fine. She glanced around and saw a heavy woolen throw. She marched over to him and took his hand.

"What are you doing?" he asked.

"Just follow me."

She dragged him over to the couch, pushed him down, then draped a throw, that was nearby, around him. "You need this. Your teeth are chattering."

"But you—"

"I'm warm now. I guess we'll have to stay here for the night and reschedule our flight back. Oh, Dr. Rollins said we need to make sure to drink lots of fluids. Let me check the kitchen to see what supplies we have."

"I have a carton of juice in my bag."

"I'll get it," she said before he could get up. Lora went to his backpack, opened a flap and saw a colorful drawing inside. "A rabbit?"

Justin had his head back and his eyes closed, but a faint smile touched his lips. "My niece drew it for me."

"Cute." She grabbed the carton she'd seen him buy at the airport, then opened the top and handed it to him. "Do you want to take a nap?"

"No." He opened his eyes and reached for the carton. "This is good, thanks."

"I'll go see if I can make coffee or something warm." Lora went into the kitchen and was thankful to see that there was enough food and drinks to sustain them for a couple of days. She really didn't like how worn Justin looked. She made a pot of coffee and returned with a cup. She watched Justin finish the carton of juice and then take the coffee and finish it, too.

He flashed her a crooked smile. "Stop that."

"Stop what?"

"You only look at me in two ways, with annoyance or concern."

"How would you like me to look at you?"

He raised a sly brow. "Do I really have to tell you?"

Lora nervously looked away and quickly turned on the TV.

An anchorwoman appeared. "We are preparing for a major blizzard to hit."

"A storm?" Lora said. "I knew I had a bad feeling about this trip. There's no way we'll get a flight out now."

They watched the forecast and learned that a snowstorm threatening to dump three to five feet of snow was headed their way that night.

"At least we have a place to stay," Justin said.

Lora stood. "True. I'll go check the rooms."

Lora leaped up the wooden staircase, passing dark, hand-painted portraits lining the walls that led to the second floor. She checked out two of the rooms upstairs, which were also decorated with dark wood paneling and antique furnishings, and decided against staying in either one. Heavy, dark brown drapes hung at the windows and piles of paper littered the ground, making it near impossible, if there were an emergency, for a quick escape in the night.

She walked farther down the hall to a quaint room overlooking the front of the house. Although it was also heavily furnished, there were no papers, and when she pulled back the thick paisley-patterned curtains, light from the setting sun flooded the room, making it appear warm. This is where she would stay. Next door was a medium-size room with an enormous king-size bed, which she decided would be perfect for Justin. While checking out the bathroom, which to her surprise had all modern fixtures, her phone buzzed. She glanced down and saw a text from Justin.

U didn't answer my question.

What question?

Do u want to forget the phone call?

She bit her lip. How should she reply? Be coy? Pretend there had never been a phone call? She paced, then finally typed two letters.

No.

Then why do we need two rooms? We could keep each other warm.

She stared at the message. Was he really saying what she thought he was saying?

I'm already warm.

"I could keep you *very* warm," a deep voice said.
She glanced up and saw Justin standing in the doorway.

"This is supposed to be a business trip," she stammered, his presence making her senses spin.

"That ended the moment the project was cancelled."

He hadn't moved from the doorway, but the room suddenly felt smaller and very intimate. Lora tugged on her collar, her gaze unable to leave his. She felt as if she was being held hostage—and she didn't mind a bit. "And what took its place?"

He crossed the room and stopped in front of her. "An opportunity to get to know each other better."

"How much better?"

He twirled a strand of her hair around his finger. "Weren't you the one who said scientists are curious?"

"They are."

He let her hair go, lowering his voice. "So aren't you curious about me?"

"I have a theory about you."

"Let's hear it."

She shook her head, aroused by his heated gaze. "No, I want to prove it or disprove it first."

"How?"

"Kiss me."

His gaze dropped to her body. "Do I get to choose where?"

She lifted his chin and tapped her mouth. "On the mouth," she said, although his sensuous look made her feel naked.

He feigned disappointment. "Just the mouth?"

"You can choose another spot later."

"Good."

When his lips touched hers, she discovered everything she had wanted to. He lips were both sweet and spicy, and they made her forget herself. Soon his kisses made a warm, wet path down her throat. "Have you proven your theory?" he asked, his breath warm against her skin.

"I'm still not sure."

"Did you bring it?" he asked, the tip of his tongue teasing her skin.

"What?"

"The robe."

"No."

He straightened and stared at her. "Why not?"

"Because I don't have one. I lied about having one."

"Hmm…I'll have to fix that." He removed her glasses and set them aside.

"Are you wearing boxers?"

"No, I'm wearing briefs, but I brought a pair."

"That will have to wait for another night."

He took her hand, led her over to the bed and gently pushed her onto her back.

"Yes. Now close your eyes and just pretend I'm a voice on the phone."

She did.

"Now I'm taking off your blouse. You feel that?"

"Oh, yes."

"And your bra, one strap at a time."

She felt his thumb brush over her nipple. "That's not my bra."

"Sorry, I got distracted. You know, you're beautiful," he said, cupping her breast.

"That's still not my bra."

"It's a lot more interesting."

"Should I open my eyes?"

"No…wait. Okay, I'm removing your bra now."

"Took you long enough."

"All we have is time. Now I'm pulling down your pants…"

Lora let herself slip under his spell as she felt him slowly remove her panties. His voice lulled her into a dream state of ecstasy. "You must have stolen your voice from the devil."

"I told you, I've been a bad boy." He kissed his way up her thigh, then licked her center. She curled her toes.

"Be as bad as you want."

"I plan to."

She soon felt his bare, warm flesh on top of hers. He was hard and smooth, and she curved into him.

Justin grabbed his trousers and pulled out a condom from his back pocket.

"You were optimistic about this trip," Lora said.

"I have plenty more in my suitcase. I have a theory of my own." He rolled on the condom, then gathered her to him.

That night, there was nothing cold about Justin. His lovemaking skills took her to a level of ecstasy she had never experienced before. His mouth and warm tongue traveled the length of her body, licking, sucking, kissing. While his hands caressed and explored every inch of her slender frame, she indulged and reveled in the pleasure. She felt like a goddess being worshiped—no man had ever made her feel this way before. She, in turn, explored his body with her hands and mouth, delighting in hearing soft sounds of pleasure escaping from him.

"You make me want you over and over," he whispered breathlessly. "I've never felt this way with any other woman before. Where did you…"

"Hush. Just enjoy," she said.

For the next few hours they immersed themselves in each other, climaxing over and over again. Lora fell asleep with a smile on her face. She later woke and looked over at him. His lashes feathered his cheek, and she lightly ran her finger over them, then his eyebrows, surprised by how quickly his face had become dear to her. She'd been so wrong about him.

Unexpectedly, her father's voice rose up in her mind. "You think you're so smart, but you're not. If you're so smart, why haven't you done anything great? Other kids make their parents rich." She blinked back tears. "I'm so sorry," she whispered.

"I know," Justin mumbled. He opened his eyes. They were clear, not hard like stone, and she wondered how she could have ever thought they were cold.

"How can you forgive me when I acted like such a fool?"

"Tonight I'd forgive you anything," he said, a lazy smile spreading on his face. Then he covered her mouth with his.

An hour later they lay in each other's arms, neither feeling sleepy, even though it was near midnight. Justin reveled in the surge of victory. *She's all mine now.* And he'd make sure that was the way it would stay. It felt so right.

"I can't believe this," Lora whispered in awe. "I can't believe we're together. I never imagined it."

I did. Many times. "Hmm."

"When I first saw you three years ago I thought—"

"I was a jerk."

"No, that you were handsome and compassionate. You had this expression on your face when you looked at Suzette that I never saw on any of the other medical staff. What were you thinking as you looked at her?"

That might be me one day. But Justin knew he couldn't say that. Not yet anyway. He didn't want her to know certain things. He didn't want to risk losing her. "I just thought that she was someone I wanted to help but couldn't. My words were callous because I wanted to put a distance between me and the situation."

"I understand," she said softly, but he could still hear a note of pain.

He caressed her cheek, wishing he could take her hurt away. "But you forced me to be human again."

"And you reminded me to be her friend."

"You taught me a lot. When you said I'd become accomplished as a scientist but failed as a man, it sliced through me."

Lora closed her eyes and groaned. "Oh, please don't repeat it. I was wrong."

"You were right. I hide behind my accomplishments. I let them prop me up and use them as a way to keep people at a distance."

"Why?"

Because I feel too much, see too much and hate feeling helpless. Because I am already an outsider and don't want to be more so.

"I was a shy kid growing up, and it just seemed easier that way."

"I know what you mean. I couldn't please my father so I stopped trying. He's never liked me, and I don't know why."

He pulled her closer. "Fortunately, I like you," he said against her throat. "I like you a lot."

The next day Lora woke up, grabbed her glasses and looked out the window to see a fresh blanket of white. "Yes, we're definitely stuck."

"At least we still have power," Justin said, seeming unconcerned. "Let's go see what we can eat."

They went into the kitchen and Lora cooked a meal of whole-wheat waffles, scrambled eggs and bacon while he set the table and washed up after her.

"There's not much in the kitchen," she said.

"I know. But this is fine with me."

"If I were at home, I could do a much better job."

"It smells great."

"But with so little to work with—"

"Lora, it's fine. I like it."

"You're not just saying that? Oh, wait…it's you."

"Exactly, I'd tell you if I didn't like it."

"And why and what I could do to improve it."

Justin shrugged. "You know me well. Personally, I would have added more spices."

She jumped up. She was always anxious about cooking for someone new. "Let me see what I can find."

He grabbed her wrist. "I was joking. It's great. Relax and eat."

After breakfast, they went back upstairs. This time, they decided to make love in the bedroom with the king-size bed. Justin stripped off Lora's clothes one by one, as if she were an early Christmas present, the mere touch of his hands sending shivers through her.

"Let's play a game of trust," Justin said as he took off his clothes.

"Trust?"

"Yes, I want to see how much you trust me."

She took a deep breath. "Okay, what do I have to do?"

"I wish I had handcuffs and a blindfold, but we'll improvise."

"With what?"

He left the room, then came back with a scarf and a fresh pair of socks. He used the scarf to blindfold her, then used the socks to tie her hands to the headboard.

"When does the fun begin?"

"Looking at you like this makes me as hard as a post."

"That wasn't my question."

"Right now. You're my captive, and my goal is to make you come like you never have before." One hand slid down her stomach to the swell of her thigh.

"That's a bold promise."

"The best kind."

His mouth covered hers with a savage mastery that made her body melt. When his body touched hers, every fiber of her being seemed to respond to him. She became aware of the scent of his skin, the feel of his mouth, the sensation of him roaming inside her and touching her sweet spot. She surrendered completely to him, her body craving more and more. She felt wet and wild and glorious. She whispered his name and moaned it as if she were a sacrifice on his altar. Finally he collapsed on her, then rolled off.

"That was…" she breathed, unable to find words to describe it.

"Yes." He untied her hands, then fell on his back.

Lora removed her makeshift blindfold. "Next time you'll be *my* slave."

"I look forward to it."

She looked over at him as he lay in bed with his arms behind his head. "Why are you smiling?"

"I just had a fantasy come true. I always wanted to be stuck in a snowstorm with a beautiful woman and spend half the day making love."

"I'm glad I could be of help."

"Do you have a fantasy?"

Lora opened her mouth, then shook her head. "It's silly."

"Tell me anyway."

"I've always wanted to pick up a man in the produce section at the supermarket, then go out into the parking lot and…you know."

"Okay. Tell me when and where."

"Really?"

"Sure, when we get back we'll meet and make your fantasy come true."

"You certainly are a man of surprises."

* * *

On the second day of their stay, Justin went on his laptop to reschedule their flight. Lora went downstairs to find something to cook for dinner. Suddenly everything went dark.

"Justin, where are you?"

"I'm in the back room. Where are you?"

"In the kitchen."

"Looks like we just lost power."

"I hope it doesn't stay off for too long. I wonder if he has a generator."

Justin made his way to the kitchen. "Let's see if we can find some candles and matches or a flashlight with batteries." They both searched all the cupboards and drawers in the kitchen. No luck. Lora decided to check a closet in the hallway.

"I've found some candles and matches," she said with triumph.

"Great."

She made her way back to the kitchen. Although the house was dark, a streetlamp and the moon provided enough light to make things visible.

"Hey, he has a small generator," Justin said, coming back inside from the back porch. "I'll go plug it in and take care of all the connections."

"Great, at least we'll be able to keep the food safe and cook a meal."

"And make a fire—or at least turn on the electric fireplace to keep us both warm." He sent her a naughty grin. "Or better yet?"

"Better yet what?"

"Have you ever made love in front of a fireplace? It would be a shame to waste the ambiance."

"Aren't you hungry?"

He took her hand and led her to the other room. "We can eat later."

Justin pinched himself. It had been the fourth time that day. He couldn't believe he was really here with Lora, having great sex, when just a few days ago… No, he didn't want to think about the past. Right now was perfect. Too perfect. He knew he couldn't go on without telling her the truth about himself. He wanted her to be a part of his life, and she had the right to know what that meant. Thank goodness he'd been able to avert a crisis when they first arrived. It had been close, but he'd recovered quickly from the dehydration and avoided a full-blown attack. He wouldn't have wanted her to see him that way. For now he felt like Superman, but he knew he was really Clark Kent.

As they sat in front of the TV watching a rerun of *The Cosby Show,* Lora curled up against him. She liked to stretch her legs out. Justin knew his current couch was too small for that, so the first thing he planned to do when he got home was buy a new one. "There's something you should know."

She rested her head on his shoulder. "Tell me anything. I'm kind of glad the project was cancelled. I'm relieved to get away from sickle cell just for a while. It's only now that I realize how much the disease has ruled my life, and that I need a break from it."

His heart fell. "Oh."

"But that doesn't matter. What were you going to say?"

"Nothing."

She sat up and looked at him. "No, I'm sorry I interrupted you. You said there's something I should know."

"My dog snores."

Lora frowned. "You thought that was important to tell me?"

"When you sleep over you might want to bring earplugs."

"I hope when I visit I won't be just sleeping."

"You'll have to sleep sometime."

She chewed her lip.

"What is it?"

"How should we act at work?"

"Like colleagues."

She nodded in agreement. "Right. We can't let our relationship affect our work."

"Yes, but I'll invite you to my office and we'll make love under the desk."

Lora laughed. "This is going to be strange. I'm so used to hating you."

He placed a kiss on her shoulder. "I'm glad I was able to change your mind."

"Me, too."

The day before their rescheduled flight back, Lora stood staring out the window. "I almost don't want to go back. I'm afraid to. This has all been so wonderful. It's like a dream, and I don't want to wake up."

"It's not a dream." Justin wrapped his arms around

her. "It's real. I'm real. And in case you don't believe me, I still think you're undisciplined."

"I know." She pushed up her glasses. "What if your sisters don't like me?"

"They will."

"Or your dog?"

"I'll replace him."

She turned her head and frowned. "That's not funny."

Justin gave her a reassuring squeeze. "He'll love you. Relax, we'll make this work."

Lora looked out the window again. "It's just that I'm scared to be this happy. Before Suzette got sick my life felt so perfect, and then it all fell apart."

"Nothing is going to happen."

She turned to him and lightly touched his face. "You mean so much to me now. I didn't expect it, but it's true. If anything happened to you, I don't know what I'd do."

Justin held her close, not knowing what to say.

Chapter 9

Fifteen days to Christmas

Minnesota already felt like a dream. Justin waited in the cafeteria line, absently picking up the items in front of him. Only two days ago he'd been alone with Lora, but now they were back in the real world. She'd offered to cook dinner for them tonight, and the day couldn't end fast enough. He paid for his meal, then sat at one of the empty tables.

Oliver took a seat in front of him. "Well?"

"Well what?"

"What happened? I heard there was a bet among the research staff that one of you wouldn't come back alive."

"We worked things out." He looked around, then lowered his voice. "She's going to cook me dinner tonight."

"That she-devil has a domestic side?"

"I told you it was a misunderstanding."

Oliver sighed. "I hope you know what you're doing."

"I do."

"At least you've found someone who understands your disease."

Justin cleared his throat. "She doesn't know yet."

"She doesn't know? Why haven't you told her?"

"I started to, but the timing wasn't right."

"There won't be a right time."

"I'll tell her soon."

Oliver paused then said, "Has she met any of your sisters yet?"

"We just got back."

"So that's a no?"

"Correct."

Oliver sat back. "She will soon."

"Why do you say that?"

"Maureen's here."

Justin spun around in his chair and saw his sister making her way toward his table. "Damn, what is she doing here? I don't know how she keeps getting past security."

"No one would dare stop her."

His sister marched up to his table. "I knew I'd find you here. You're like clockwork."

"What do you want?"

She kicked his chair. "Why won't you answer your phone? We've been worried sick about you. Ann told me you were acting weird at dinner last week, then you're off to Minnesota, get caught in a snowstorm and come back without returning any calls, forcing me to come here to see if you're still alive."

"As you can see, I'm fine."

"You should have called."

"I'm sorry."

"He's been preoccupied," Oliver said. "By the new woman in his life."

Maureen took a seat, smiling. "New woman? What new woman?"

Justin sent Oliver a look. "It's nothing."

"She'd find out eventually," Oliver said.

"Find out what?" Maureen asked.

Justin sighed, knowing there was no recourse. "I'm seeing someone."

"A colleague," Oliver added.

"Someone who works here?" She stood. "I have to meet her."

"She's not here today," Justin said.

"You're lying."

"Go home."

"I'm going to find her."

"No, you won't."

"I'm not leaving until I meet her."

"I'll show you a picture one day."

"Stop being stubborn. I won't embarrass you. I just want to see what she's like. Oliver, help me."

"You'll meet her later," Justin said. "But not here. Now go home. I'll call you tonight, I promise."

"You'd better, or next time I'll bring Sarah and Ann with me." She kissed him on the cheek and left.

"You enjoyed doing that, didn't you?" Justin said to his friend.

"I'll do worse if you don't tell Lora the truth. Find the time to tell her."

* * *

Warren needed a new plan. He sat in Union Station wondering what he should do next. Justin hadn't been disciplined by Oliver, as he'd hoped would happen. Instead of being reprimanded and blamed for Lora's inappropriate outburst, nothing had happened. And Lora was still in her position. He'd have to get in Rollins's good graces another way. He'd tried to butter him up as much as he could while Silver and Lora were in Minnesota, but it hadn't worked. He sighed.

"Why such a heavy sigh?" a female voice said.

Warren glanced up, ready to tell the woman to leave him alone, but once he saw her, all words fell away. She was a woman who could give him a hard-on the size of a missile. She was gorgeous, with a face meant for fantasies and a body that inspired wet dreams.

"Just thinking about work," he said. "I'm a lead scientist working on a special treatment for sickle cell anemia, and one of our patients just passed away." He did his best to look devastated.

She took the seat next to him. "Oh, that's awful. You poor man." She lightly touched his thigh.

He wished her hand would move higher, but he'd wait for that. Right now he just needed a name and a number. "Yes, it's been hard." He held out his hand. "I'm Dr. Rappaport."

"Sylvia Turner," she said.

Minutes later, he had a number and address and a date to meet again. Warren had gone to Union Station for lunch and to think. When he left, he felt much better than he'd expected to.

* * *

Sylvia watched Warren leave with a sense of satisfaction. She was going to enjoy this assignment. She still remembered her conversation with Belinda, who she'd met several years ago when she'd pulled an elaborate con game on Belinda's greedy ex-husband. Sylvia hadn't known he was married—he'd sworn he wasn't—and her informant (a former private investigator with a hustler's love for money) had been sloppy. After conning him out of $100,000, she'd discovered the truth. She'd felt badly that his wife had suffered, too.

She'd sent Belinda half of her earnings—anonymously—but she somehow found her. And the moment they met, they became instant friends. Belinda got rid of her cheating, conniving husband and gained a friend. Ironically, Sylvia gained something she usually didn't have—someone she could trust. She had associates who helped her with her cons, but her circle was small—it was safer that way. So when Belinda asked for her help, she knew she couldn't refuse. Sylvia waited until Warren was out of sight before she dialed. "Hey Belinda," she said. "I just met with that Rappaport guy. Poor Lora. I can see why she fell for him. He's very charming."

"I don't care," Belinda said impatiently. "Did it work?"

"Oh, yes, he's completely hooked."

"Good. He has to learn his lesson."

"Don't worry, Belinda. I'll give him one he won't forget."

* * *

What had she been thinking? Lora wondered for the twentieth time as she dusted and polished her apartment in preparation for Justin's visit.

Their flight back from Minnesota had been uneventful. They hadn't been able to get seats together, again, and had separated at the airport parking lot.

"Well, I'll see you at work," she'd said.

"Only at work?"

"Uh…no, you could come over for dinner."

"Sounds good. I'll bring the wine."

Now she found herself rushing around her apartment hoping to make it man-ready. A single man hadn't entered in years. She wanted to show sophistication, so her collection of teddy bears dressed up as doctors and scientists went inside her bedroom closet. She grabbed a fitted cream-colored silk blouse and a knee-length black leather skirt that showed off her figure, from her closet, and she fixed her hair while the dinner simmered. She then put on a hint of eye makeup but painted her lips a deep cherry red. She wanted them to say "kiss me" without her saying a word. By the time the doorbell rang, she was ready. She swung the door open with a smile and got the reaction she wanted. Justin stared, mesmerized. "Hello," she said.

"Hello," he said in a husky voice.

"Do you want to come in?"

He shook his head a little, as if trying to focus, and held up two bottles. "I didn't ask if you wanted red or white so I bought both."

"That's perfect." She took the bottles from him and opened the door wider.

He stepped inside, then turned to her. "Right now I think I'm staring at perfection." He pulled her to him and kissed her.

"I don't want the dinner to burn," she whispered against his lips.

He reluctantly released her. "All right." He sniffed the air. "Something smells good."

"Thank you. Dinner's just about ready. Please take a seat." She pointed to her dining room.

He kissed her once more, then went to sit.

Lora caught him looking around her place but couldn't read his face clearly. It was annoying that he was able to mask his emotions. She really wanted to impress Justin and had gone out of her way. She had made a plate of spiced meat patties, fried plantains and baked zucchini with sautéed red onions. When Lora was growing up, her mother had made sure she could cook some basic West Indian dishes, just in case she ended up marrying a man from "back home." Little did her mother know that if Lora married, she didn't expect to cook much but instead planned on having her meals cooked by a personal chef or de-livered.

Justin ate with evident enjoyment. Finally he set his utensils down and sat back. "The food was amaz-ing. I love Caribbean cooking."

Lora beamed. "Thank you." She fell quiet, then said, "But there's something you don't like."

"I didn't say that."

"When you looked around my apartment what did you see?"

"You have a very nice place."

"But it's not organized enough?"

Justin started to look uncomfortable. "It doesn't matter what I think."

"But I want to know."

He sighed. "Okay. Why don't you have any decorations?"

"What?" Lora thought his comment odd coming from him—his office was so sparsely decorated.

"It's ten days before Christmas, and you wouldn't know it from looking at your place."

"Oh, I don't really celebrate Christmas."

"Why?"

"It was never a really big deal at home."

"But you're an adult now. We only have so many holidays to celebrate. You don't even have a pathetic Charlie Brown Christmas tree."

"A Charlie Brown what?"

"Like the tree featured in the cartoon holiday special."

"I've never seen it."

He stared at her for a moment, as if waiting for a punch line. "Really?"

"Nope."

"How about the movie *It's a Wonderful Life?*"

"A wonderful what?"

"Life. It's a classic holiday film."

"What's it about?"

Justin stood. "No, I can't have my girlfriend living like this." He checked his watch. "It's only eight-thirty. Get your coat."

"Where are we going?"

"Shopping. A lot of the stores have extended hours, so we'll be fine."

He took Lora to a local general gardening store, where he bought her a small holly bush and a miniature tree, taking the time to get the one with the freshest scent. He also bought several boxes of tiny white Christmas lights, an assortment of glass-blown ornaments and a nutcracker. They went to an entertainment store and picked up several holiday DVDs. Back at her apartment, they decorated the holly bush, which went outside and then strung lights around the balcony while holiday music played softly in the background. Once finished, they stepped back to admire their work.

"That's better," Justin said.

"Thank you."

"Now it's movie time. It's a tradition in my family. We choose a film every holiday season and sit around watching while eating caramel popcorn and gingerbread cookies."

"Sounds nice."

"What are your holiday memories?"

Lora remembered her Dad shouting. Her mother in tears while she and her sister tried to stay quiet to avoid being in the line of fire of their father's acid tongue. There were no holiday lights or sweets. "I don't have any. My parents were usually working. I have nothing to complain about."

"Tell me you've seen *A Christmas Carol*."

For her, the holidays meant forced family gatherings where her father's anger ruled. Everyone trembled in his wake. He thought Christmas was foolishness and let everyone know. They had a tree, but no ornaments. He didn't allow gifts, saying it was Jesus' birthday, not theirs. Her mother stayed silent. There was no real joy or brightness at this time. As a child, most of the time after breakfast, she would go over to Suzette's house and spend time with her and her mother until it was time for the holiday dinner, which was once again dominated by her father's presence.

"No, but I did see *Scrooged* and thought it was hilarious."

"Not quite the same thing. Well, I'm going to fix that. We're watching that movie tonight." After *A Christmas Carol* they watched *A Charlie Brown Christmas,* and the movie didn't end until 4:30 a.m. They decided to call in sick that day, make love, spend more time with each other and watch *A Christmas Story* and *It's a Wonderful Life.*

Lora loved all the movies and teared up during the scene in *It's a Wonderful Life* where George Bailey is at the bar praying to God. She cheered at the end when the town came to his rescue.

"I wish someone had found out what that awful Potter did."

"Doesn't matter. Real wealth is knowing who your true family and friends are."

She groaned. "I almost forgot."

"What?"

"This weekend is my family's holiday party."

"When?"

"This Saturday."

"I can make it."

"I'm not sure you should." She'd worked hard to get a date just for the event to show off, but now she didn't want to."

"I'd really like to meet your family."

"Okay."

Maybe this time it would be different.

Chapter 10

Lora looked into her new compact mirror and applied more lipstick. She didn't usually check her makeup, or wear any for that matter, especially when she went grocery shopping, but today was special. She looked around the supermarket. If she was going to pick up a man, she had to look her best. She spotted Justin in the produce section pretending to look at the apples. She only had to walk over to him and say something. Boy, was he handsome. She seemed to notice it more and more every day. It was sweet of him to help make her fantasy come true. She put her compact away, straightened her back and walked toward him.

She knew it should be easy, but she suddenly felt shy and awkward. She hadn't expected so many people to be around. What if someone overheard? But it wouldn't be fair to have him come all the way there and not try.

Anyway, it was just for fun. She took a deep breath, smoothed her hair and walked over to him.

"You know, the best way to choose an apple is to smell it, right where the stem is," she said. "If you smell a fragrance, it usually means it's sweet."

"Really? I didn't know that."

"I also know a great recipe you can try once you find the right ones."

"I'm not much of a cook."

"I'd be more than willing to help."

"If you want something easy," a female voice purred, "I have a few tips." Another woman appeared next to Justin and lightly touched his sleeve.

Lora looked at her unexpected competition. She was an attractive brunette with light blue eyes and a body that could distract anyone. She wore a red jacket trimmed with white, making her look like one of Santa's naughty elves.

Justin turned to her and smiled. "Oh, thanks, but—"

Lora walked in front of him. "Back off."

"Why should I?" the woman asked. "It's a free country."

"Because he's mine."

"You might have seen him first, honey, but that doesn't stop me from reeling him in."

"Cast your net somewhere else because you're going home empty."

The woman looked up at Justin. "That's for him to decide."

"I'm making the choice for him."

She held up her hands in surrender. "Fine." She

winked at Justin. "Happy holidays," she said as she turned away.

"Yes," Lora sneered. "Ho, ho, ho."

The woman spun around, her eyes blazing at the innuendo. "What did you say?"

Justin covered Lora's mouth. "She didn't say anything."

The woman shot her a venomous glance as she walked away.

Lora removed Justin's hand. "That woman ruined everything." She turned to Justin and saw him bite his lip. "You think this is funny?"

He shook his head, but his chin trembled.

"It's not funny," she said.

He turned his back to her, and she saw his shoulders shake.

"Stop laughing."

He sent her a glance over his shoulder. "Ho, ho, ho?" he said between breaths. "You're vicious."

"I suppose that was a little juvenile."

He laughed harder.

"You're really enjoying this."

He grinned. "I should go shopping more."

"She ruined my fantasy."

"We can still have sex in the parking lot if you want."

"It's too cold."

"I could keep the car running."

"No. That wouldn't be smart or safe. We could die of carbon monoxide poisoning. I could just imagine the news report," she teased, knowing that couldn't really happen.

A light twinkled in his eyes. "Yes, but what a way to die."

"Try to be serious."

"I'm always serious. Wait right here. I'm going to pick up a few things." He left.

Lora chose several plantains, annoyed. Damn—all that buildup for nothing. They could always try again, but she wasn't sure she'd be in the mood.

"You know I never know how to cook those," a deep voice said behind her.

She glanced up and saw a good-looking man staring at the plantain with confusion. "Oh, it's really easy. First you have to make sure it's ripe enough. You don't want it to be too soft or too brown or bruised. It should be firm with a little give, deep yellow with few brown spots."

He stepped closer. "And then what do I do?"

"The best part. Fry them, bake them or steam them."

"Sounds complicated. Do you think you could show me?"

"No, she couldn't," Justin said.

The man looked at him and then at Lora.

"Sorry," Lora said, attempting to soften Justin's cutting tone.

"Thanks for the tip," the man said as he walked away.

Lora turned to Justin. "What was that? You nearly made him jump out of his skin."

Justin smiled. "That was my intention."

"So you can flirt, and I can't?"

He raised a brow. "I wasn't flirting."

"You were enjoying the attention of that woman, and I was enjoying the attention of that man."

"Now you have my undivided attention," Justin said with a teasing look "What are you going to do with it?"

Lora playfully grabbed his collar. "Come with me. I have a few ideas."

A few days later Lora's spirits weren't so buoyant. She felt a sense of dread as she and Justin drove to her family's holiday party. The word "party" seemed liked a misnomer. Instead it would likely be her father insulting someone and her mother and various relatives trying to pry into her private life. At least now they wouldn't pity her.

Her plan had worked but not the way she'd expected it to. She wasn't spending the holidays alone and she finally had someone to take with her to the family gathering. She was in control this time. But that knowledge didn't stop her from trembling inside.

"You're quiet," Justin said. "Are you nervous?"

"Yes."

"Why? You don't think they'll like me?"

"No, it's not you." *It's me,* she silently added. She wanted the evening to be perfect.

"Then what is it?"

"I just want you to enjoy yourself."

"I will."

That would be a miracle. "My family's not always very friendly. Especially my father."

He squeezed her hand. "It'll be fine."

Unfortunately, her mother had set out to prove him wrong. She opened the door dressed in a fitted grey outfit more suited to a woman with three times her income and flashed a polite, plastic smile. "I was wondering if you two would ever show up." Her words were short and snappy, making her sound like a displeased English headmistress.

Lora stepped inside and took off her coat. "I didn't mean to be late."

"I suppose I can't blame you. I guess you wanted to make a special entrance to show off your new man."

"No—"

"You can blame me for the delay," Justin said. "I'm sorry if I've caused any trouble. It's a pleasure to meet you."

Lora's mother smiled. "The pleasure's all mine. I'm Grace." She wrapped her hands around his arm and led him away. Lora went into the kitchen, where she found her sister.

"Can I help?"

"No, I've got things under control. What's the name of your date again?"

"Justin Silver."

"Wait…the guy you hate?"

"I don't hate him anymore."

Belinda looked past her toward the kitchen door. "So where is he?"

"In Mom's clutches."

"Poor man." She handed Lora a tray. "I'd better go rescue him." Belinda rushed out of the kitchen before Lora could stop her. She sighed. She should have been prepared for this, but even she hadn't expected such an obvious display of interest. She left the kitchen with the food tray and saw Justin talking to her mother, her sister and a cousin. She held out her tray. "Mushroom tarts, anyone?"

Her mother touched a finger to her forehead as if in pain. "Are you trying to embarrass me?"

"Belinda handed me the tray—"

"To put down," her sister said. "Not to serve."

"That's okay," Justin said, reaching for one. "They look delicious."

"I made them myself." Belinda said.

"Along with Betty Crocker," her cousin snorted.

"I followed the instructions."

"Wonderful," Justin said.

"Put the tray down," her mother said.

"Fine, I'll be right back."

"Just set it over there."

"It's not a big deal."

"You're a guest and should act like one. Do you want Justin to think I treat you like a servant?"

"I'm sure you're a wonderful mother," Justin said.

"I try my best, but sometimes I wonder."

Lora bit back a groan.

"Hello," her father said as he joined them. It was uncharacteristic of him to greet anyone. "You must be Belinda's new man," he continued, his island accent heavy.

"No," Justin corrected. "I'm here with Lora."

"Lora?" He sent his younger daughter a dismissive look. "Why? You're a good-looking man, so what would you want with her?"

"Stop joking," her mother said with an uncomfortable laugh. "Justin's not used to your humor."

"Who says I'm joking?"

"Lora doesn't have many male friends," her mother said quickly.

"She doesn't have *any*," her father said in a flat tone. "You're the first she's ever brought over to meet us. She thinks she's better than everyone because she's got a bunch of letters after her name. How did you meet her?"

"We work together."

"That's good. I'm sure they do background checks where you work. The classifieds and those things on-line are full of scammers and liars."

"Not all, Dad," Lora said.

"Did I say all? You're just lucky you haven't fallen for one of them."

"Come on, Dad. Let's not argue," Belinda said.

"I'm not. I'm just stating fact. How come every time I talk to your sister you think I'm arguing? Is she so thin-skinned? Do you think we should all be impressed because she brought this man here? Will we meet another one next year?"

Justin looked at Lora. "Get your coat, Lora."

"What?"

"We're leaving."

Mrs. Rice gasped. "But you just got here."

Her father laughed. "You're as soft as she is."

"Apologize," her mother pleaded to her father.

"Why should I? It's my house. I'll say what I want."

"You're embarrassing me," her mother said as Justin helped Lora with her coat.

"I'm sorry, Mom," Lora said.

Justin shook his head. "Blame me, Mrs. Rice." He opened the door.

"Does she pay you by the hour?" her father called after him. "I guess she couldn't afford more than a half hour."

Justin spun around, and Lora saw his eyes flash fire. She grabbed his arm and tried to drag him out the door. "Let's go, please."

"Let me just say one word," he said under his voice.

"You'll regret it."

"No, I won't."

"Please."

He stared at her then nodded and turned.

Lora waved at her stunned family before closing the door.

They got in his car and drove in silence. It was worse than she could have imagined. Couldn't they have pretended to be proud of her instead of making it all a cruel joke? Were they really so ashamed of her? She was glad Justin wanted to leave so that he could drop her home and she could go into her room and cry.

"I guess you must think I'm a liar," Justin said.

She turned to him surprised. "No, why?"

"I didn't handle your parents well. I don't like your father, and it appears the feeling is mutual."

"I'm sorry about that."

"You have nothing to apologize for."

"I know." She sniffed and wiped away a tear.

Justin swore fiercely. "He made you cry? That's it—I'm going back."

Lora grabbed his arm before he could make a U-turn. "No, don't, please. It's not worth it. I don't want to go back."

"I hate to see you cry."

"I'll stop in a minute."

He pulled the car over to the side, parked and gathered her into his arms. "I didn't realize…" His words fell away.

"They were that bad? I should have prepared you."

"I wouldn't have believed you." He stroked her back. "Please stop crying."

"I didn't think it would hurt so much. I don't mind when they do that in front of strangers or when it's just family but to behave that way in front of you? I'm so embarrassed."

"That's your mother talking. There's nothing to be embarrassed about." He brushed her hair from her face. "Are you sure you weren't adopted?"

She laughed. "I'm not. I checked."

He glanced at his watch. "There still might be time."

"For what?" she sniffed, suddenly feeling better. Her family hadn't driven him away. That meant something.

"I want you to meet my sisters."

"I can't meet them yet."

"Why not?"

"I've just been crying."

"You look fine. Besides, by the time we get there your eyes won't be so red and puffy."

She shot him a glare. "Thanks."

He grinned. "You'll like them."

"I hope they'll like me."

"They don't have a choice."

Chapter 11

A half hour later Lora stared up at a house aglow with Christmas lights. Everything looked so homey. She already knew that his family celebrated the holidays in a big way, so what if she didn't fit in? She stopped at the walkway.

Justin turned to her. "What's wrong?"

Lora searched inside her purse for her phone. "I'm calling a cab."

He seized her hand. "No, you're not." He pulled her along.

"We can do this another day. They're not even expecting us. Are you sure they like surprises?"

He rang the doorbell. "Yes."

"You're hurting me."

"No, I'm not."

"If you let me go, I won't run away."

"I don't believe you."

She made a face.

He laughed and rang the bell again. "You're going to thank me for this."

The door swung open and a short woman with dimples and a wide smile stood there. Her hair was braided and pulled back. She wiped her hands on her apron, which covered her full figure, and hugged him. "Justin, what a surprise!"

"This is my girlfriend, Lora. Lora, this is my sister Ann."

"Nice to meet you, Lora. This is great! We can always use more hands in the kitchen." She turned and hurried down the hall. "Come on in."

Lora turned to Justin. "More hands for what? I'm not the best chef."

"You're a great cook." He gently shoved her in front of him. "Relax. Don't you trust me?" Before she could say no, he bent down and kissed her. "That's what I thought."

He led her into the kitchen. On the table were cookie sheets and cutters, and the scent of vanilla and sugar filled the air.

"It's great to have you here, Lora," another woman said, shaking her hand. "I'm Maureen and that's Sarah. "The way our brother goes on about you we thought he'd made you up."

Unlike with her family, Lora could tell their teasing wasn't mean-spirited.

"You look all dressed up. Where did you two come from?"

Lora opened her mouth, not sure what to say.

Justin rested a protective arm around her shoulders. "We briefly visited her family," he said in a terse voice that invited no questions. His sisters took the hint and said nothing.

Maureen wisely changed the topic and put Lora and Justin to work. Lora was soon having more fun than she ever thought possible. Within minutes she felt like one of the family as she talked and laughed with them. Ann talked about her daughters, who were at a sleepover, Maureen discussed her recent vacation to the Cayman Islands and her current boyfriend, while Sarah talked about her flower shop. This was how a family should be, Lora realized.

Once the cookies were all out of the oven and cooling, they all gathered in the family room. Sarah sat next to Lora but Justin stood in front of them. "Move."

"No, I want to talk to Lora."

He lifted his sister and moved her, then he sat down beside Lora. "She's mine." He winked at Lora and she blushed.

"I'm so glad Justin has found a woman like you. Interested in sickle cell disease, especially because he—"

"—is so interested in it, too," Justin interrupted.

Maureen narrowed her eyes. "Yes," she said slowly.

"How long have you been seeing each other?" Sarah asked, changing the subject.

"Almost two weeks," Justin said. "Not long."

"It's long enough."

"A woman should know everything about the man she's seeing," Maureen said.

"Lora knows plenty."

"I'm still learning," Lora said with a nervous laugh, not understanding the sudden tension. "Justin is full of surprises."

"Right now our little brother is full of something."

"Maureen, be fair," Sarah said. "It's too soon."

Lora leaned forward. "I don't know what's going on, but if I've done something—"

"It's not you," Justin said.

Maureen stood. "Justin, help me bring out the cookies."

He sighed then followed her into the kitchen.

"You haven't told her?" Maureen said once she and Justin were alone.

"Not yet."

"Why not?"

"It's too soon. I'll tell her after the holidays."

"She really likes you. I don't see that changing."

"Her friend died from complications of sickle cell anemia. I was there. I'm not sure she's ready to be close with someone like that again."

Maureen shook her head and sighed. "You sure know how to pick them. First that girl who dumped you after you had a crisis, and now her."

"She's different."

"Then prove it. Tell her tonight and see if she'll stick around."

"I don't need to prove anything to you. I know her, and I know what I'm doing."

"You deserve a woman who loves you no matter what. Like we do. If she can't handle the truth about you, then it's best to know that now."

"She can handle it. Just give her time. Right now she needs me. If you'd met her family you'd understand. She needs to create happy memories and good times. I want to give them to her."

"At what price? Does she know she can't push you too hard? That you can't—"

"I'm taking care of it."

"I don't like this. I—" Maureen stopped when they heard a light knock on the door as Sarah entered.

"What's taking you two so long?" she demanded. "Lora is already beginning to suspect something."

"Don't you think Justin should tell her the truth?"

"This isn't up for discussion," Justin said, heading for the door.

"It's important," Sarah said.

"I didn't say it wasn't. If you want us to leave, we will."

Sarah grabbed his hand. "We don't want that."

"She just had a bad experience with her family and I won't expose her to another."

"We don't want that, do we?" Sarah said turning to Maureen.

Maureen folded her arms. "I still don't like it."

"I like her."

Maureen sighed. "I do, too, which is why—"

"You should let me deal with things my way," Justin finished.

"All right."

"Good, that's settled," Sarah said. "Now we have to come up with a reason for our disappearance."

"I already have one. Stop looking so worried," Justin said. He left the kitchen and returned to his seat beside Lora, who had been chatting with Ann. "What's going on?"

"We were just discussing where you are going to spend Christmas. But I wasn't sure you'd go for it."

"What?"

"We'd like you to spend it with us," Sarah said, catching on. "If you want."

"I'd love to. Thank you."

On the trip home, Lora couldn't stop raving about his sisters. "You all get on so well. I mean Maureen seems a little fierce at times, but I really like her and Sarah and Ann."

"And they like you."

"I can't believe I'll get to spend time with you, your sisters and your parents."

"You'll love it. You'll spend Christmas Eve and then wake up and open gifts, and you'll get to see what the day can really be like."

"What do you want for Christmas?" Lora asked.

"You wrapped in a ribbon lying under the tree."

"Besides that."

"Okay, you don't have to be under the tree. You can be on my bed."

"Be serious."

"I am. I'm not that hard to please."

"That's okay. I already have an idea and I have four days to figure out how to get it."

This was only their fifth date together, but it seemed like Carla had known Griffin a lifetime. She was helping Griffin complete his Christmas shopping, and with only his daughter and his mother and father to buy for, it was simple. Carla thoroughly enjoyed showing him some of her secrets to shopping so that he could minimize his spending but get items that would impress.

Once they were finished shopping, as part of their routine, they would go back to Carla's apartment for a cup of hot chocolate and biscuits. Ariel had gotten used to Carla's place and was perfectly content amusing herself with the selection of baby toys that surrounded her in her playpen. Carla had decided to buy one for when Griffin came to visit.

"You know, you're beginning to grow on me," Griffin said as they sat in front of her fireplace.

"Same with you. I hope you haven't made any plans for Christmas because I'd love to spend it with you."

"Me, too."

"Come over on Christmas Eve. I'll cook a special dinner for you."

Neither knew at that moment that his stay would last through the New Year.

Lora was finishing her breakfast that Sunday morning when Belinda called. "You are in so much trouble. I don't know if Mom and Dad will ever forgive you."

"I didn't do anything."

"You left with him."

"He was my date."

"You can make it up on Christmas Day."

Lora hesitated.

Belinda pounced. "What is it?"

"I won't be there," she said in a rush.

"What do you mean?"

Lora adjusted her glasses, gaining courage. "I won't be spending this Christmas with you. Justin's family invited me to spend time with them."

"You'll have to say no."

"I already said yes."

"But we always spend Christmas together."

"And we're always miserable," Lora added. "Dad hates the holidays and lets everyone know it. Mom will be disappointed with the gifts we give her, although she'll pretend to be pleased—"

"I know it's not fun, but it's family. At least Dad allows gift giving now that we're grown. It's tradition, and family always comes first. What if you and Justin don't work out? He may not be around next year, but you have us forever. I'm not saying it'll be easy, but it's what you're supposed to do."

"I'll see everyone on New Year's Eve."

"You're making a mistake."

"It wouldn't be the first time."

Although Lora said the words, the guilt still lingered in her mind days later as she lay with Justin in Ann's guest bedroom. It was the night before Christmas and too late to turn back now. She wondered what she would do if all her joy faded away.

Lora slipped out of bed and went downstairs to the living room, where the large tree was still lit. Brightly colored presents sat underneath. Six red Christmas stockings hung by the fireplace, and fresh fern draped the mantel. Ann really went all out for the holiday. She had even exchanged the throw cushions on the couch with red and gold ones and the bathroom now had holiday towels and a Christmas rug, along with pine cones and scented candles.

Lora sat on the couch and looked around in wonder. It was like a dream. She'd already met Ann's husband and her two daughters, Monique and Jayla, when she'd first arrived. Monique was the oldest at seven, and Jayla had just turned three. Tomorrow Justin's parents would arrive. As wonderful and welcome as they made her feel, she knew they belonged to Justin, not her. What if their relationship didn't make it to next year? Would another woman be sitting here? Would she be forced back to the bickering and the sadness of spending Christmas with her family?

The joy she felt scared her. And her feelings for Justin scared her because her love for him had become a part of her. How could she make sure it never went away? That he never went away?

"Waiting for Santa?"

She quickly wiped away tears. "No."

Justin sat beside her and gathered her close. "Hey, hey, what's wrong?"

"Nothing," she said with a little laugh. She pushed up her glasses. "I'm just so happy. It's incredible. I've never been this happy during the holidays."

"I'm glad." Justin pulled her to her feet. "Let's start a tradition all our own." He led her over to the mistletoe. "Starting now, we'll kiss under the mistletoe every Christmas Eve." He lowered his lips to hers.

Lora kissed him back, her heart jubilant. If he was thinking of next Christmas, that meant he saw a future with her.

Chapter 12

It was like one of the holiday movies they'd watched. Lora gazed in awe as the Silver family opened gifts and hugged and kissed each other with delight.

She opened her gift from Justin: a red silk robe. She'd gotten him season tickets for the Baltimore Ravens.

She saw the delight on Monique's face when she opened her Digital Dilly. She raced over to her uncle and gave him a big kiss on the cheek. Monique was nothing like Warren had described. Unlike her younger sister, Monique was reserved and quiet but polite. She'd greeted Lora with a soft greeting but Lora hadn't found it off putting. And as time passed the little girl warmed up to her, offering her shy smiles.

"Ms. Lora," she said. "You haven't opened any more of your gifts."

"I don't have any more. The one from your uncle is enough for me."

The little girl frowned and looked at the remaining packages under the tree. "But there's a bunch more here for you." She picked one up and handed it to her. "See? It has your name on it."

"But I didn't get anyone else gifts."

"Doesn't matter," Justin said. "Just open them."

"Who are they from?"

Lora read the label. "Maureen."

"But I didn't get anything," Maureen said.

Sarah nudged her. "Yes, you did. Remember, we went shopping."

"Oh, right."

Lora opened the present and found a purple woolen scarf. "This is amazing. Thank you all so much."

She also received a new set of dish towels from Ann, an expensive bottle of perfume from Sarah and a slow cooker from his parents.

Lora looked at all the gifts. "I don't know what to say. I can't thank you enough."

"We're so happy you're here," Ann said, clearing up the used wrapping paper strewn around.

Once all the presents had been opened, Justin went to help Monique set up her Digital Dilly account and Mr. and Mrs. Silver went to the den to watch a holiday movie. Ann went to prepare lunch, and Lora went into the bathroom in the hallway to wash her hands when she overheard Maureen talking to Sarah.

"Did you know that Justin was going to do that with the gifts?" she said. "Pretend that they were from us?"

"Yes, and I helped him."

"My God, how much did he spend?"

"It doesn't matter."

"Shouldn't she know he planned everything? She needs to know what a great guy she has."

"She does. Stop being so suspicious. She's not like the other one."

"It's like he's buying her affections because—"

"He cares about her. There's nothing more to it."

"Still, I think he should tell her."

"Maureen, be quiet."

"I can't believe everyone's agreed to keep it a secret from her. Even Mom and Dad. I think it's a terrible deception."

Lora came out from hiding. "What should I know?"

The two sisters turned to her, stunned.

"It's something for Justin to tell you."

"Is it bad?"

"Depends on how you view it."

"Just tell me."

"It's not our place to," Sarah said. "Ask him."

Lora waited for lunch to end and then motioned to Justin to follow her into the den. "What aren't you telling me?"

"What?"

"I overheard your sisters Sarah and Maureen talking about you."

He swore. "Let's talk about this later."

"I want to talk about it now."

"I want this day to be perfect for you. Please, let's talk tomorrow."

"No."

He sat back and sighed. "I was going to tell you… Damn, this is harder than I thought."

"Just say it."

"I have sickle cell anemia."

Lora shook her head. "No, you don't."

"Yes, I do."

"How bad?"

"Severe."

"And how old are you?"

"Thirty-six."

"Congratulations. When was your last crisis?"

"Lora, don't do this to me. Don't treat me like I'm a disease. I'm still the same man."

"No, you're not. Excuse me." She raced out of the room.

Justin didn't follow her; he just sat in a daze. His perfect day had gone all wrong. His sisters approached him.

"Did you tell her?" Ann asked.

He nodded. "Yes, and she left the room."

Maureen folded her arms. "Fine, then you can return all those gifts. I hope you kept the receipts."

"Maureen, have a heart," Sarah said. "Can't you tell he's upset?"

"It's better he found out about her now."

"I'm fine," Justin said in a hollow voice.

"You're not fine," Ann said. "And I think I should go talk to her."

Justin stood. "No, don't do that. I'll talk to her." Justin went upstairs to the bedroom they shared, not knowing what he should say. Would he be met with anger? Disdain? Could he explain why he'd deceived her? He had to prepare himself for her cutting remarks. He stood in the doorway and watched Lora rummage through her suitcase.

He leaned against the door frame, feeling as if he had no strength left. She was leaving him. "If you want me to take you home, I will."

She shook her head. "I don't want to go home yet."

He straightened, surprised and hopeful. "You don't?"

"No." She upended her suitcase, then searched through the contents. "I don't know why I can't find it."

Justin cautiously walked toward her. She didn't look angry. "But…aren't you upset with me?"

She stared at him, confused. "Should I be?"

"Yes. Downstairs you left because I'm not the man you thought I was."

"Careful. Are you about to jump to conclusions?"

"I don't understand."

Lora smiled. "You're right. I'm not being fair. Oh, here it is." She came around the bed and stood in front of him. "It's true. You're not the man I thought you were. You're even more remarkable than I thought. I wanted to find something to show you." She opened his palm and placed a stone inside. "I was going to give it to you along with your gift, then I changed my mind. But I think you deserve it. It's a good-luck stone given to warriors before they set out to battle. I've always thought of you as a warrior, and now I know I was right. I admire you more than ever."

"As a man or as a scientist?"

"Both," Lora said as she hugged him and held him close, trying to ignore the whisper of fear that swept over her heart.

Chapter 13

A fierce early-March wind pounded against the café windows. Carla barely noticed it as she sat inside nursing her drink. *So this is what love feels like,* she thought as she watched Griffin get a refill of his coffee. She glanced down at Ariel, who was asleep in her stroller. How had this happened? How had she become so attached to them so quickly? Her relationship with Griffin was still a marvel to her. They were different in so many ways—she was more take-charge, and he was more laid-back. He liked leisurely drives; she liked having a destination. He was a father; she'd never even thought of having kids.

Yet they got on well. She'd known him now for three months, and after the play they attended in December, they hadn't been able to get enough of each other. They never ran out of things to say. She loved being with him. No matter how stressful her day was, Griffin made her forget it all. For Valentine's Day he'd given her a diamond sapphire bracelet, which she thought was a very risky move, considering they hadn't been dating long. But she'd accepted the bracelet and wore it every day.

She knew he'd be leaving the café soon to drop Ariel off at the babysitter before he went to class. She wished there was a way she could guess where their relationship was heading. They'd held hands and he'd kissed her on several occasions, but she still wasn't sure he felt the same way about her as she did him. As an older woman, she held firm to ninety days before sex, but most men didn't last that long. So far he had. She had also grown close to Ariel. She loved playing with her, and Griffin had been so pleased when she'd offered one day to braid Ariel's hair. And when they went to a toy store, she'd loved watching Ariel's excitement and awe looking at all the toys and stuffed animals. Of course, Carla had bought her two large stuffed bears—she couldn't resist. But now she wanted him to become a bigger part of her life. So far he'd been somewhat of a secret—never meeting any of her family or friends. But she was ready to change that. She'd asked him to attend the ground-breaking ceremony for the new pain clinic project next Thursday afternoon and he said he would come. It was a start.

Griffin returned to the table and grabbed the jacket he'd thrown over the back of his chair. "I really wish I didn't have to go yet."

Carla stood and helped him with his collar. "It's

okay," she said. Both of them had busy schedules—his busier than hers—and savored the time they were able to squeeze in to be together.

He caught her hand and looked at her bracelet. "I wish I could have gotten you something flashier."

"I don't need flashy." She smiled at him. "I love it."

He kissed her, and not with one of the light feathery kisses he'd given her in the past. This was something more—the kiss of a man who wanted a woman. It was quick but intense and full of meaning. When he drew away his eyes burned and at that moment Carla knew he felt the same way she did. If they'd been alone she would have stripped him naked and had her way with him. They were definitely ready for the next level.

His gaze searched hers. "Carla?"

"Yes, I want it, too," she said, answering his silent question.

Griffin released a sigh of relief. "It's just the timing."

"We'll make time."

"Is that a promise?"

"Don't you trust me?"

He kissed her again. "Yes," he said. "I really want this to work."

"It will."

He bit his lip. "I don't want to go."

"But you have to."

"I could skip class."

"You're paying too much money to do that. Now go."

"All right." He took Ariel's stroller and reluctantly left.

Carla sat down hard on her seat, tasting his kiss

on her lips. Yes, she was in love, and she wouldn't fight it. It was a wonderful feeling. She glanced up, and her heart stopped when she spotted Lora's sister, Belinda, sitting at the counter staring at her. Carla inwardly groaned. *Bullet Belinda,* as Lora called her, would no doubt have an opinion on what she'd just seen. Belinda made her way over to Carla's table.

"Who was that?" Belinda asked in a stage whisper.

"A friend," Carla said, sipping her now cold coffee.

"You looked like more than friends," she said, sliding into a seat. "Lora didn't tell me you were seeing someone."

"She doesn't know."

"Is he supposed to be a secret or something?"

"He's my business, that's all."

"Is he babysitting or something?"

"No, he has a daughter."

"You're dating a child with a child," she said, laughing at her own attempt at humor. "Is that wise?"

"Belinda—"

"I mean, that's a lot of baggage. You have your career to think about. I'm all for having fun, you know that. And a woman your age has a right to treat herself and throw caution to the wind, but if I were to get a boy toy he would be without accessories."

"He's not that young. And the age difference isn't that big."

Belinda shrugged. "If you say so."

Carla felt herself getting angry. Who was Belinda to judge? Who was anyone? She liked her life, and she liked him. No, she loved him. Was that so wrong? Was she really taking on more than she could handle?

She hated that Belinda had forced her to ask herself questions she didn't want to face but knew she had to.

Lora sat in front of her parents at their dining table, realizing that her peace offering wasn't going to be enough. She'd brought dinner to their house and told them the news she'd been eager to share: she'd won the Pointdexter Fellowship. She'd worked hard for it, and now her dream of funding had come true. After finding out about Justin's disease, she felt more certain than ever about her proposed research and its importance. She wanted to help him. Cure him. Give him the life he deserved. None of the current treatments had been able to work a hundred percent, but maybe hers would. Now that he'd hired a new team leader they rarely saw each other at work. Fortunately, they made plenty of time for each other after hours.

She hadn't told Justin yet about the fellowship, although she was sure he already knew. He was probably disappointed. But at that moment she wished she'd chosen Justin's disappointment to her father's scorn.

"And you came over here to lord it over us, did you?" her father said, his West Indian island lilt even more pronounced.

"I thought that for one time in your life you'd be proud," she said.

"Proud of what? It has nothing to do with us."

"We are proud," her mother said.

"Where's that man you brought with you last time? Gone already?"

Lora clasped her hands. "I'm still seeing him."

"That must be a record for you."

Lora sighed. She didn't know why she thought telling her father about the award would change anything. She thought of calling Carla, but getting hold of her outside of work had been difficult lately.

"I guess I should go."

"You're not going to stay for dessert?" her mother asked, sadness written on her face.

Dinner had been a struggle enough. "No, I have to run an errand."

Her father folded his arms and leaned back in his seat. "She's got a big fellowship now. She doesn't need us."

"That's not true."

"Why did you let that man shame us like that?"

"Because you were being rude."

"I was stating my opinions. That's not being rude. If he were a real man, he could have taken it."

Lora stood and left. She knew she couldn't win an argument with her father. For some reason, he liked picking fights with others. Growing up, she kept Suzette away from her parents as much as she could. Although she loved her mother, at times she wondered what she saw in her father to have married him. Her mother had grown up in a middle-class household in a nice area and gone to a prestigious boarding school. Upon graduation, at the tender age of seventeen, she had met Bernard Rice and he had swept her off her feet.

Her mother's family hadn't been supportive of their relationship, but her mother had been so in love, she eloped and that was that. Her father had only finished sixth grade and hadn't had an opportunity to go back to school. As the youngest of eleven children, he had literally been used as a slave to his brothers and sisters in Port Antonio, Jamaica. When he was pulled out of school, he was sent to the country, where he'd lived with his older sister and helped her take care of her five children. He was later forced to work in his brother's poultry business. He'd worked long hours, seven days a week, without getting paid. Resentment had made him bitter at a very young age. When he'd turned eighteen, he ran away to Kingston where he worked in a factory. He had found different jobs here and there before finally getting an apprenticeship as a painter.

"Bernard, why must you treat your daughter so?" Grace asked, gathering up the dirty dishes once Lora had gone.

"I don't treat her any different than I treat others."

"You know that's not true."

"Woman, what do you know?"

"I know that you resent her achievements because you always see yourself in her and know her life and success could have and should have been yours." Tears gathered in her eyes as she saw the strained look on her husband's face. Although he hadn't been able to complete formal schooling, he was a very bright man, and given the opportunity, he would have gone far.

"I remember wanting to be a doctor when I grew up," he said, his voice almost wistful. "I had so many dreams. I would finish high school, go to university then medical school and then open a medical practice. And I could have, if my family had recognized

my ability and supported me. But no one saw me beyond someone they could use for their own gain. I
didn't exist to them. Except for Thelma—she was the
only one there for me." He remembered his sister with
fondness. She'd been the second born and had treated
him more like her child than her brother. She never
married, and for the first five years of his life, she'd
spoiled him and taken care of him. Unfortunately,
she'd fallen ill and died, and he had to return home.
"Bernard, it's time you moved on. You have made a
good life for yourself and your family. You need to
stop seeing yourself in your children, especially Lora.
One day you won't be here. How would you like her
to remember you? As you remember your father, or
as something better?"

"I'm a good man."

"I know. But you have two wonderful daughters.
Not just one. You must love them equally."

"I know that. Why do you think you have to tell
me what I already know?"

"Because you only see one. The other one you treat
like a pariah. She did nothing to be treated this way,
except for the fact that she has brains, does well in
school and excels at whatever she does. Bernard, it's
time you let go of false dreams, embrace the children
you have and be proud of them."

A half hour later Lora was at Justin's door. She
knocked and then heard Louis barking.

"Who is it?" a deep, raspy voice asked.

"Lora."

She heard him swear.

She took a step back, shocked and hurt by the response. "I could come back another time."

"No, it's not because of you." She heard the locks disengage and then the door opened. The man who stood before her looked awful. He had the rough makings of a beard and deep circles under his eyes. "It's just that now is not a good time."

Lora knew the signs of a sickle cell crisis. "Why didn't you call me?" she demanded, pushing her way past him. "What have you taken? Where does it hurt? Why aren't you lying down?"

Justin closed the door then rested against it. "One question at a time."

"Forget it. Lie down." She went over to help him. "You can lean on me."

He held out his hand. "No, I'm too heavy." He pushed himself from the door and started to limp over to the couch. But the quick movement was too much for him and he started to pitch forward. Lora rushed over to grab him before he hit the ground. But he was too heavy for her so she stumbled back and fell, managing to soften his fall. She gently pushed Justin off her. He'd passed out. She scrambled to her feet and tried to drag him over to his couch. Unfortunately, he was too big and heavy for her to lift up, so she grabbed a small cushion off the couch and placed it under his head. She then put a blanket over him. She glanced at his side table and saw a small prescription bottle. She read the label. It was a strong narcotic, and she knew it would definitely do the trick. He would be knocked out for several hours.

Lora knelt next to Justin, knowing there wasn't

more she could do for him. He needed to rest and wait for the pain medication to take effect. In the meantime she'd take Louis for a walk. Lora got Louis's leash and put it on him, but the dog didn't want to leave Justin's side. She tugged on his collar. "We'll be back."

Her words and tone seemed to reassure him. Louis licked his master's hand then wagged his tail enthusiastically to tell Lora that he was ready to go outside.

Where am I? Justin opened his eyes and stared up at the ceiling. Why was he on the ground? The last thing he remembered, he was on his bed trying to get through a crisis. Wait. He had answered the door for Lora, but that was the last thing he could recall. What had happened? Justin sat up and swore. He hoped he hadn't passed out on her. He'd hate for her to see him that way. God, he hoped it wasn't that. Where was Louis?

He slowly rose to his feet. At least he felt better.

"Careful or you might fall."

He spun around at her voice, lost his balance and fell onto the couch.

Lora walked over to him. "Glad the couch caught you this time instead of me."

"What happened?"

"You had a crisis."

"I know that, but how did I end up on the floor?"

Lora bent down and lifted his jeans leg.

Justin swatted her hand away. "Stop that."

"I just want to check for any swelling," she said, sounding hurt.

He softened his tone. "There isn't any."

"You're going to need another day of bed rest."

She was right; he still felt drowsy. "I know. So what happened?"

"You tripped and fell."

Justin narrowed his eyes. "You're lying to me."

She grinned. "Yes, do you want to hear the truth?"

"No."

"Then lie down and rest some more."

Justin sank into the cushions, already feeling his limbs grow heavy. "You'd better still be here when I wake up."

"Is that a request or a demand?"

A wish, Justin thought as he drifted off to sleep.

Chapter 14

I must be dreaming, Lora thought. The guard at the front desk at the lab had said her mother was waiting for her in the visiting area. Her mother never visited her. Something had to be wrong. Lora raced down the stairs, not bothering to wait for the elevators. She pushed through the first-floor doors and spotted her mother sitting calmly near one of the windows. Lora could see she'd dressed with special care, and her hair was impeccable. She looked as if she were applying for a job instead of coming to meet her daughter.

Her mother turned and stood when she saw her. Lora rushed up to her.

"Mom, what are you doing here?" she asked, trying to catch her breath.

"Why are you breathless?" Grace retorted.

"When the guard at the front desk told me you

were here, I ran down the stairs. What's the emergency?"

"There's no emergency."

"Then why are you here? Is something wrong?"

"Why? Must there be something wrong for me to visit my own daughter?"

"No, but..."

"But what?"

"I mean, you've never visited me at work before. You've never even expressed interest."

"So, I guess you think I'm too old to change." She turned, ready to leave.

Lora grabbed her mother's arm. "No, it just that I was surprised. It's wonderful to see you."

Grace sat like a queen indulging a peasant. "So, do you have the time to show me what you do?"

Lora cringed. She was in the middle of writing a proposal that was due in two days, and no, she really didn't have the time. But she wasn't going to tell her mother. They rode the elevator to the second floor, where Lora's lab was located. Lora introduced Grace to the other members of her staff and later took her to meet Carla.

They went to the cafeteria, and Lora ordered a cup of hot tea and a chicken sandwich for her mother.

"So, is this what you do all day?" Grace said with interest.

"Yes, I'm looking for ways to make people with sickle cell anemia live longer, pain-free lives."

"Do you work with white rats and such, like they show on TV?"

"No. Most of my research involves looking at what

current treatments are available and analyzing why some work for some and not for others, so I study data taken from live subjects. Human beings, not animals."

"I see." Then her mother paused. "I wanted to apologize for the way your father behaved when you brought that young man to visit. What's his name again?"

"Justin. Dr. Justin Silver. And you don't have to apologize for Dad."

"But I do."

"Mom, I'm used to Dad by now."

"You may be, but I'm not going to tolerate him shaming you anymore."

Lora was too shocked to speak. Her mother, although not a wallflower, had never approached her like this. Lora shifted, uncomfortable with her mother being so honest.

"Justin was right to leave," her mother continued. "Yes, your father was offended, but that was the first time I have ever seen anyone let him know that his behavior, at times, is unacceptable." She adjusted her hair. "As for me, I was disappointed. I so wanted this holiday gathering to be without the typical insults your father is used to throwing at you. Lora, I know I don't always say it, but I love you. I am proud of you, and you mean a lot to us. We are so proud of what you have done." She grabbed a napkin to dab at her eyes. Lora knew her mother hated to cry, especially where anyone could see. "When you came and told us that you won that scholarship, my heart jumped for joy, but as usual, your father doused my enthusiasm. I couldn't say much. Don't hate him."

"I don't hate him." Lora shrugged. "But I've always known that Belinda's his favorite."

"You'd have a right to hate him. But he loves you. He just can't show it."

Lora didn't fully believe her mother but was touched that she had taken the time to tell her. "Mom, I love you and Dad very much."

"Are you still seeing your young man?"

Lora grinned at her mother's formal tone. "Yes."

"Perhaps I can see him again for lunch or something?"

"It's a date," she said, and to her delight her mother smiled.

Carla glanced at her watch, her heart sinking. *He wasn't going to make it.* It was already 11:45, the groundbreaking ceremony was well under way and Griffin hadn't shown up yet. Didn't he know how much this day meant to her? Did he even care?

Lora sidled up to her. "You keep checking your watch. Are you bored already?"

Carla thought of lying, then decided against it. "No, I was expecting someone."

"Oh, yes, Belinda told me you're seeing someone. I'm happy for you. She's says he's a real cutie. Good for you." She looked at Carla's outfit. "Wow, you look fantastic. You must really like this guy."

Carla blushed. She had taken a lot of time to get ready for the event. She had bought a new ivory two-piece suit with an embroidered trim and a pair of lime-green sling-back heels, and she was wearing a very expensive pair of stockings. The skirt had a side

slit that allowed it to fall at the perfect angle to em-
phasize her shapely legs. She had also had her hair
colored to cover up her few strands of gray.

"Thanks," Carla said. "I'd better go and see what's
keeping him. Excuse me." She moved away from the
crowd and dialed his number.

A sleepy voice picked up. "Hello?"

"Griffin, where are you?"

"Hi, Carla. I'm in bed. Why?"

She sighed. "You forgot."

"Forgot about what?"

"The groundbreaking ceremony."

Griffin swore, suddenly sounding wide awake.
"Carla, I'm so sorry. I crammed to get a paper in
and then had to work and Ariel had a bad night, so I
totally forgot. I don't think I'll be able to get a babysitter but—"

"Forget it."

"I'm truly sorry."

"Me, too."

"I'll make it up to you."

"You don't have to. Get some sleep." She hung up
before he could reply. Perhaps this was a sign. They
both had different lives and different obligations. She
didn't want to pull on him. She'd wanted him to meet
Lora and see her world, but perhaps this was how it
was supposed to be.

Chapter 15

The dog park bustled with the sound of happy dogs playing and owners chatting while the early-June sun beat down on them. Justin threw Louis a yellow Frisbee, which he easily caught and brought back to him. It had been more than a month since his mini crisis and he felt better than ever.

He handed Lora the Frisbee. "So when are you going to tell me you won the fellowship?"

Lora looked at him, unsure. "I didn't think you'd want to talk about it."

"Why?"

"I beat you."

Louis barked.

Lora glanced down and realized she was still holding the Frisbee he was waiting for. "Sorry about that, Louis," she said as she threw it to for him to chase.

"I know you beat me." Justin rested his hand on his chest and winced, pretending he was in pain. "And I've been waiting weeks for you to make me feel better." His smoldering gaze skimmed over her body.

A grin touched the corner of her mouth. "Are you heartbroken?"

"Devastated."

She pressed her lips against his. "I'm sorry to hear that," she whispered against his lips. "What would you like me to do?"

"Anything you want."

She laughed. "I'll think of something." She bent and petted Louis when he dropped the disc at her feet. "Are you really upset?" she asked, avoiding Justin's gaze.

"No. I'm proud of you. Congratulations."

"Don't say it if you don't mean it."

He frowned. "I do."

"You'd be the first."

"What do you mean?"

"Nothing." She tossed the Frisbee as far as she could.

"No, tell me."

"Except for Carla and Dr. Rollins, you're the only person to congratulate me. Everyone thinks you should have won. And my father…" She shook her head. "The less said about him the better." Belinda hadn't said anything special, either, except for "Congrats," but Lora never expected much from her sister, who had never valued academics. Besides, she had promised herself that she'd never be like her father and hold resentment. She accepted her sister for who she was—her sister loved her and that was all that mattered. She wished she could accept her father in the same way.

Justin gripped his hand into a fist. "I think your father and I should have a talk."

"It wouldn't change anything."

"I can be very persuasive."

She took his hand. "Forget about him. Come on, let's go home."

"I'm not ready to go home yet."

"We've been out here more than an hour and you're sweating. At least let's go get you something to drink."

Justin gritted his teeth. "I'm fine. You don't need to baby me. I have my parents and sisters to do that."

Ever since his crisis, she'd become noticeably concerned about his health. At times she fussed over him as if she were his doctor instead of his girlfriend. He hated it. He wished she hadn't seen him that way. He wished she didn't look at him with worry in her eyes. He wanted her to look at him as though she thought he was strong. Someone she could depend on. Someone who would protect her. Instead, she acted as if she needed to protect him.

"I just care about you," Lora said in a soft voice.

"I know, but you don't need to tell me what to do. I can handle it."

She sighed. "You're deluding yourself."

"What?"

"You push yourself too hard. I mean, you just had to train the new team leader. Last week you conducted two lectures at two different universities. We've come to the dog park every day this week and you haven't been sleeping because of that grant deadline."

"So what?"

"You can't overexert yourself. Stress is dangerous for you. You need to get plenty of rest, drink lots of fluids—"

"Are you going to give me a prescription for folic acid supplements, too?" he sneered.

"They help," she snapped. "You know that better than anyone. Why are you fighting me on this? I'm not the enemy."

Louis barked.

"Quiet," Justin said. Louis sat back on his hind legs, looking up at the pair with apprehension. "I don't need you constantly reminding me of this disease. If I want to drink fluids, I'll drink fluids. If I want to do ten lecture tours, I will."

"Why? Why are you so driven to try to outdo everyone? You're only thirty-six. You've accomplished so much already, so why do you keep pushing yourself?"

Because sometimes I feel as if I'm on borrowed time, he wanted to shout. Instead he kept his voice level and said, "I'm ambitious. And I don't want to talk about this anymore."

"You never want to talk about it. Why do you want to pretend that you don't have it? You take careless risks. Like the trip to Minnesota. The flight and the cold really could have done a number on you."

"I managed. And don't tell me you regret it." He shot her a significant look.

"That's not the point."

"Look, it's my disease, not yours. So let's drop the subject."

"As a couple—"

"We should respect each other."

Lora threw up her hands. "Fine." She turned. "If you don't want to go home, I will."

Justin watched her go, making no move to stop her. He then picked up Louis's toy and threw it with extra force. She didn't understand. He wanted to live life on his terms. He didn't want to be a slave to his disease. He knew she worried about him because of what had happened to her friend, but he didn't want that baggage between them. He'd beaten many odds. He wanted her to believe he'd make it, too.

The man was infuriating! Lora thought as she entered her apartment. She didn't understand why he was so stubborn. Just like Suzette had been at times. That was what frightened her most—he was too proud to admit his weaknesses. He kept doing things that could be harmful, as if he were trying to make her see that he was like any other man. But he wasn't. She wished she could do something to make him see it. But was she being too much of a nag? The issue seemed to loom larger and larger every day. She'd gone to get checked to see if she carried the gene, and luckily, she didn't. But they'd never discussed having a family. Was she really making it a bigger deal than she should have? Lora sat on her couch and sighed. The fear continued to grow, and she didn't know how to stop it.

* * *

Carla sipped her wine as she studied Griffin across the table. She'd treated him to dinner at an expensive Italian restaurant, and he'd responded as if she'd given him a new car. He was so easy to please, so easy to be with. She loved just looking at him, at his warm brown eyes and broad shoulders. He looked as if he could carry the world, but she knew he was only human. And it was time for her to let him go. She'd chosen the elegant atmosphere because she imagined it would be the perfect place for their final goodbye.

He smiled at her. "You're right. The food here is delicious. I know of a seafood place we should try next." He winked at her. "But I'll pay next time."

She set her wine glass down. "Griffin, I don't think there should be a next time."

He paused. "What do you mean?" He set his utensils down. "Are you still angry with me about the groundbreaking ceremony? I'm really sorry I missed it and—"

"I'm not angry. I just see that right now we have two very different lives."

"Carla—"

"You have your work and school and your daughter," she continued in a rush, not wanting him to convince her otherwise. "I have a new research project I need to focus on, and I don't think we should add a relationship on top of that. You're young."

Griffin narrowed his eyes and lowered his voice. "Don't make seven years sound like a generation gap. And don't make it an excuse. My age was never a problem before. Address the real issue—I screwed up and missed something important to you. I won't make that mistake again."

"You didn't make a mistake. You made the right choice. I think you should find a woman who can help you, not demand more of you."

"I don't need help. I just—"

"I think we need some time apart to think things over."

"I don't need to think. I already know that I love you. I guess the real question is, do you love me?"

Carla shook her head. "That doesn't matter. Love isn't enough."

"How about respect? Admiration? Devotion? Isn't that enough?"

She shook her head, unable to answer. Tears choked her. He was an idealist, she was a realist and she wanted him to see that they had too much against them to make it work.

Griffin pushed himself away from the table and stood. "Fine. I'll give you the space you want. Goodbye."

Carla closed her eyes against building tears as she listened to him walk away.

Chapter 16

Warren was roused out of a deep sleep by a ringing phone. Who would be calling him on his landline at this time of the night? He thought of disconnecting the line, then saw the number and answered. It was Sylvia. Beautiful Sylvia with legs up to her neck. Perhaps she was feeling lonely tonight and wanted company. He picked up the line. "Hey, babe."

"He knows."

Warren sat up as fear coursed through him. After their first encounter he'd learned that she was married—all the better because married woman didn't expect much—but they'd been careful. "How?"

"Someone has been following us. He has pictures. I've sent them to your cell phone."

Warren scrambled out of bed and grabbed his cell phone. He stared at the pictures with growing panic.

These were clear pictures of him in compromising positions with Sylvia. Someone had been watching them very closely. He flipped through the images, then stopped at the last image. It was a scribbled note that said: you're dead.

Warren swore and rubbed his chin. What was he going to do? How was he going to get out of this? He'd messed up. But he hadn't been able to resist the rush of screwing the wife of some big shot. She had mentioned once that if her husband ever found out about them, he was a dead man, but he hadn't worried. He'd enjoyed the sex too much for that. Now hearing Sylvia's tense voice on the phone, he wished he'd found another woman.

"Warren?" Sylvia said.

He picked the landline back up and sat on his bed. "What should I do?"

"You need to leave the area right away."

"I can't just get up and leave like that. I have a job, obligations and…"

"Do you want to live? If you don't disappear, my husband will have you killed. The note is not an empty threat. This isn't the first time."

"What do you mean?"

"The last man I was with was found floating in the Potomac."

"Oh, God."

"But I might be able to do something and—" Suddenly a rough male voice came on the line. "Is that you, Rappaport?"

His throat closed.

Warren's silence didn't stop the man. "I'm not happy with you. You've been messing with my wife, but I'm ready to be generous. I won't send my boys to break your legs. I'll give you a week to come up with fifty thousand. That's a discount."

"But I don't have fifty thousand dollars."

"You have a week or you'll be seeing me. And believe me, you don't want that to happen." The man hung up.

Warren threw down the phone and paced. He had to come up with fifty thousand dollars or he was a dead man.

A letter. Lora looked at the envelope, amazed. She couldn't remember the last time she'd gotten a letter, let alone one from her father. He never wrote letters. Lora looked at the envelope, fighting anxiety. What could it be about? Lora tentatively opened the folded piece of paper and began to read:

I'm not good at saying what I feel. I don't expect you to understand, but although I don't always show it, I am proud of you. I am proud of all that you have done. Your mother and I could not have wanted more from a daughter. Forgive me for not being able to say it to you, but at times things are difficult for me. You have done well for yourself and achieved all that you have dreamed of. In spite of the person I am, I am your father. You are my daughter.

Yours,
Father

Lora's hands trembled so badly she had to put the letter down and sit at her kitchen table. She smoothed the letter out and reread it while tears rolled down her face. Her father was proud of her. He loved her…

She rushed over to the phone and dialed her parents' number. "Mom, is Dad there?" she asked.

"Just a moment." She heard her mother call her father to the phone.

"Yes?" her father said.

Her heart was pounding, but this time it wasn't from fear but joy. "Dad, I got the letter. Thank you so much."

"Is all right," he said, sounding embarrassed.

"I love you."

"I must go," he said in a choked voice. "Here's your mother."

Her mother picked up the phone. "Is everything all right?"

"Yes," Lora said with a laugh, wiping away tears of joy. "It's wonderful. Bye." Lora hung up the phone.

She was filled with happiness. Today was a new day; they would start afresh and get to know each other. Her father had finally told her he was proud of her. She'd been waiting all of her life to hear him say those words. She held the letter close to her chest and danced.

Justin stumbled into his apartment, feeling as if he were being both stabbed and burned alive. His legs barely supported him as he hugged the wall for support. He'd had a hectic day at work, and for hours he'd been fighting a headache that threatened to flatten him. He still hadn't had a chance to talk to Lora about their argument and that worried him. And having to deal with Warren hadn't improved his day.

Warren had come into his office looking desperate. "You need to help me," he said.

Justin shook his head, then immediately regretted the movement. He'd taken several pain medications, but they hadn't started working yet. "No, I don't."

"But you're the only one who can help me. I messed up, man. This woman I met recently, we'd been seeing each other for a while, and then I found out she's married."

"That's never stopped you before."

"I know, but her husband is bad news."

"Again, that's nothing new."

"He's B. K. Turner."

"Who's B. K. Turner?"

"A very wealthy man in DC."

"So what's the problem?"

"He's also a member of a crime family. He found out about my affair with his wife and now he's put a bounty on my head!"

Justin nodded as if considering the seriousness of Warren's predicament. "That is a problem. But I told you I wouldn't cover for you again."

"Do you want Lora to know about you?"

Justin stood and came from around his desk. "She already does." He folded his arms, amused. "Try again." He was relieved that Lora knew his secret and Warren couldn't blackmail him anymore. Keeping his disease from others, especially those he worked with, had been important to him, and when Warren had seen him have a crisis, he had made him promise not to tell anyone. That had been a mistake, but Justin didn't care now.

"Look, this will be the last time."

"I doubt it."

Warren grabbed his collar and shoved Justin against the desk. "You owe me."

Justin shoved him away. "I don't owe you anything."

"You can't do this to me, man. I know you have fifty thousand you can give me. If not that, then I just need some money so I can, you know, disappear for a while. Don't you know of a lab somewhere, where I can get a position and stay out of circulation for a while?"

"Explain to me why I should help you. Or, for that matter, why I should care."

"Come on, man. I'm sure you have connections abroad. I could go to Jamaica or Antigua until things cool down." He was nearly yelling with desperation. "What do you want from me? I'm scared and need your help."

"I want you to get out of my office and handle your problems like a man."

Warren pounded the wall, then stormed out. Justin had called Oliver to tell him he was calling it a day, but he'd barely made it home. It was as if the confrontation with Warren had drained any energy left in him. Justin glanced around his apartment, relieved he'd made it home safely. He just needed to get to his medicine and combat the pain.

He clawed at his collar, trying to loosen it. He couldn't get enough air. God, why couldn't he breathe?

Why was everything so blurry? He heard Louis barking but couldn't register why it sounded as if it were coming from the end of a tunnel. He took a few halting steps forward then lost consciousness and fell to the ground. This time, no one was there to catch him.

Chapter 17

She hadn't been able to reach him, which was odd. Was he avoiding her calls? It had been three days since the discussion at the dog park, and they hadn't spoken. When she'd spotted Warren storming out of his office she'd wanted to know what had happened. Justin wouldn't answer his office or cell phone, and now his home phone kept going to voice mail. Perhaps he'd gotten involved in work. She was surprised and disappointed not to see him at his desk. She saw Dr. Rollins in the hall and asked, "Where's Ju— Uh, Dr. Silver? I haven't been able to reach him."

"He went home early."

"He wasn't feeling well?"

"He didn't say."

"He won't answer his phone."

"That's how he is."

But something seemed wrong. Justin would say she was jumping to conclusions, but she had an instinct that he was in trouble. She sent him an email and then a text but received no reply. She dialed Maureen, knowing she was the closest person to Justin's apartment.

"Hello?" Maureen said.

"Hi, Maureen. This is going to sound crazy, but could you check on Justin for me?"

"What happened?"

"I'm not sure. I haven't spoken to him for a while, and I've called all his numbers and get no reply. I know he'll think I'm just bugging him so I thought if you—"

"Right. I'll go check on him."

After hanging up, Lora could barely concentrate. Would Justin be furious with her? Say that she was meddling in his life? It was a risk she was willing to take. When an hour passed without a call back from Maureen, Lora began to relax. It was probably nothing. Maureen likely was reading him the riot act for not getting in touch with anyone. Lora was walking to her car when her phone rang.

"Hello?"

"Lora?" Ann said in a strained voice. "You've got to come to the hospital fast."

She froze. "The hospital?"

"It's bad. The worst it's been in a while. Hurry. He may not make it this time."

Not again. Not again. Lora kept repeating the words as she sped to the hospital. Ann was just overreacting, she tried to convince herself. It wasn't going to be that bad. They'd stabilize him and then everything would be fine.

At the hospital, memories began flooding back. Suzette's mother calling her in the middle of the day and telling her that Suzette probably wouldn't make it through the night. She remembered the hospital's sanitized smell. Only two days earlier Suzette had been sitting up in bed, eating what looked to be a nonpalatable plate of meatloaf, mashed potatoes and greens. She had bought several new CDs, and she and Suzette had spent several hours listening to the music while doing a crossword puzzle. When she had left, Suzette was sleeping soundly. Nothing had prepared her for the call from her mother.

Lora registered with the front desk then raced to Justin's hospital room. She halted in the doorway when she saw Justin hooked up to a ventilator. He had tubes attached to him everywhere. *Please God,* she prayed silently, *please don't take him. Not Justin.*

Ann rushed over and hugged her. "Thank God you're here."

Lora was too stunned to hug her back. "What happened?"

"I'm glad you called me," Maureen said. She sat near the wall, her face pale. "By the time I'd gotten to his place a tenant had already called the ambulance. It seems that Louis had gone crazy, and he had somehow reached the front doorknob and gotten out of the apartment. He started running up and down the halls barking and alerting everyone. A neighbor found Justin and called 911. He hasn't regained consciousness.

"He was running a fever of 104 degrees. They were

concerned that the bacterial infection he had would lead to either pneumonia or meningitis. Thankfully, that didn't happen. They put him on a major antibiotic treatment protocol, but there is still some concern. He may have also suffered a mild seizure, and the doctors won't know what damage this may have caused until he regains consciousness. No one knows how long he was unconscious and how much time passed without adequate oxygen."

Before Lora could respond, the head doctor, a woman in her fifties, introduced herself to them.

"Good morning. I'm Dr. Chin." She then turned and began discussing Justin's case to the group of residents following her. It was eerily similar to Suzette's last hospital visit. She couldn't go through this again. She wouldn't.

"Not now," Lora said to the doctor.

Dr. Chin bristled at her tone. "We're just going to—"

"I said not now! You can use someone else as a study subject. Not him. Now get out!"

The doctors hurried from the room. Lora stared at the door with satisfaction, then turned and looked at Justin's sisters. They stared back at her in horror. Her sense of victory faded. What was she doing? She sounded like a crazy person, and maybe she was. Maybe she'd finally snapped. This was a nightmare, and she had to get out. But not before telling Justin how she felt. She walked over to his bed. "I'm not going to be like your sisters and feel sorry for you. You did this to yourself because you're arrogant and stubborn. You once called me selfish and now I'll say the same to you. You're selfish because you do whatever you want, no matter who it hurts.

"You don't care how helpless we feel." She tapped her chest. "How helpless *I* feel. I can't make your pain stop. I can't save you. I thought we had a future together—I wanted a future with you, but you don't think about tomorrow. You only think about now. So I'll say this to you now. I love you. I probably always will, and I pray you'll recover from this and find the woman who is right for you. Because it's not me. You deserve so much more than this." She kissed his forehead. "Goodbye." She turned quickly, not seeing the stream of tears that slipped from under his eyelids. All she saw were the white walls and the white floors, and she knew she needed to get out of there fast.

She ran out of the hospital and down the street until her lungs threatened to burst. No. No. She couldn't do this again. They'd met in a hospital and now things would end there. She couldn't deal with it. She couldn't face the pain again. She wouldn't. He did this to himself. He wouldn't listen to anyone. To her. And now he'd... No, she wouldn't think about it. Why was the world so cruel to give her someone to love and then take him away? She collapsed onto the hard ground, feeling numb. Her fears had come true. All her happiness had been ripped from her.

Lora didn't know how long she sat staring at cars passing, but when the sun started to set she returned to her car. She started to drive home, then decided to go back to her office. Once there, she grabbed a cardboard box and started packing. She had to leave. She was giving up. Sickle cell had won. It would always win. One day someone would find a cure, but it wouldn't be her. She was sick of the disease—sick of how it stole away young lives. Maybe her father had been wrong, and she was no daughter to be proud of. She hadn't been able to help anyone she loved.

"Lora, what are you doing?"

She looked up and saw Carla. "What are you doing here? I thought everyone had gone home."

"I had a few things to do. What's going on?"

"I'm quitting."

"Why?"

"Because I'm no use to anyone."

"That's not true. You won the fellowship and you have a bright future in research. Do you know how many scientists, young and old, applied for and would have liked to have won it and the $150,000 dollars? You are bright, and you have new and progressive ideas. If I were your age and had won a prestigious award like that, I'd be on top of the world. You'll be able to really begin looking at some of those theories and treatment protocols you've been anxious to investigate."

"Who cares? They're only theories and…nothing applicable."

"In time—"

"I don't have time."

"What's going on?"

"Justin's in the hospital. He has sickle cell anemia and he suffered a major crisis while he was home alone. I don't know what I'll do if…"

Carla fell into a chair. "I didn't know."

"Most people don't. He acts as if by denying the disease he doesn't really have it. He doesn't need me. He made that clear. He wants to live his life any way he wants to, and I won't stand in his way. When you really love someone you let them go, right?"

Carla nodded, understanding more than Lora could imagine. "But I think you're being hasty. You love your work here and you *do* make a difference."

"Not enough of a difference."

"You're reasoning with your heart instead of your head."

"If he dies…I won't be able to stand the sight of his empty office or someone coming and taking his place. And if he lives…I won't be able to face the fact that we'll never be together."

Carla stood and set the box on the ground. "Come on. I think we both need a drink."

Minutes later the two women sat at a bar with a couple of pina coladas and a bowl of cashews.

"So when will I meet the man you're seeing?" Lora asked, trying desperately to forget the memories in her head. She wanted to erase the image of Justin lying helpless in the hospital bed. She needed to get as far away from him as she could.

Carla shook her head. "You won't. It's over."

"Really? Why?"

"I don't want to talk about it. We came here to drown our troubles, not talk about them."

Lora ignored her. "Is it because he didn't show up for the ceremony or because he has a child?"

Carla took a big gulp of her drink, then sighed. "Both."

"The past several months you've been very happy. If he's the reason, I'd say fight for it. Sometimes love can be messy."

Carla flashed an ironic grin. "I saw you running away from it."

Lora shook her head. "I'm different. I'm through with love."

"You don't mean that."

"Did your man ever tell you he loved you?"

"Yes."

"Justin never has. And today I learned that no matter how much I love him, he doesn't love me enough to care about how I feel."

"He's a difficult man to understand."

"Maybe one day he'll find a woman who understands him. But I'm going to stop trying. He has a family who loves him. Me? I just have a broken heart. And a career I need to focus on." She raised her glass. "To being single."

"I think you should be with him, Lora. If something were to happen…"

Tears threatened to fall, but Lora held them back. "I've already said goodbye."

It had been agony. Lora had been so close. He'd heard her voice, but he hadn't been able to do anything. Justin felt as if his heart would burst. He'd wanted to tell her how sorry he was; he'd wanted to hold her, but he was a prisoner in his body. He knew once she was gone, she'd never return. She'd said she'd loved him. Then why had she left? Why couldn't she understand he hadn't done this to hurt her? He hadn't wanted to hurt anyone; he just wanted to be like everybody else. And she was wrong. He loved her.

Chapter 18

"I'd say it was a miracle," Dr. Chin said, looking over Justin's chart. It had been a week since his hospitalization and he'd greatly improved. He'd averted severe complications from the major kidney and bone infections he'd developed. But Dr. Chin had spoken with him, at length, about the need to take his disease seriously, or the next time he may not be so lucky. "We came very close to losing you, but I'm glad we didn't." She smiled as she left. Justin was released three days later.

Maureen had come to take him home. She rested her hands on her hips. "You scared the hell out of us."

"I'm sorry."

Oliver walked into the hospital room. "You should tell that to Lora."

"I know. That's if she'll ever see me again." Justin

forced a smile. "Maybe she'd come back if I told her I could make her a rich widow."

Sarah frowned. "That's not funny."

"I'd rather see you laugh than cry."

"I think it's good she's gone," Sarah said. "She said such hurtful things. If Lora really cared about you the way she should, she'd be here. You're a great guy and if she can't see past this, then she really doesn't deserve you."

Justin shook his head. "You don't understand. She had a friend—"

"I don't care."

"And her family is—"

"That's your problem, little brother," Ann interrupted. "You're always thinking about other people. You're concerned about her and the people at work and not thinking about yourself. You can't afford to. You need someone who will think about you, who will take care of you."

"And Lora let you down," Sarah said.

"No, she didn't," Maureen said.

Everyone turned to her. "What?" Sarah asked.

"She was right. We've coddled Justin. We've forgiven him for being self-indulgent while we pull out our hair with worry. In truth, Lora said everything I wish I could say."

"But—"

"You didn't hear her on the phone. She called me when she couldn't get in touch with Justin. The way I see it, she's been hurt enough and doesn't need to be hurt again by us or anyone."

"You can't blame Justin," Ann said.

"Yes, I can. Because he knows how to prevent this. I'm not saying it will never happen again, but he can and should take measures to do something before it gets this bad."

Oliver looked at the three women. "Could you give us a minute?"

They nodded and left. Oliver sat near the bed and sighed. "Your worst fear came true, didn't it?"

Justin folded his arms, refusing to respond.

"For once, stop being so proud. You messed up. You have to face that."

Justin looked out the window.

Oliver grabbed his chin and forced him to look at him. "Do you want to see your next birthday? Do you want to have a family of your own one day? Then you need to act as if you have a tomorrow instead of living each day as if it were your last. You can't pretend any longer. You have to face your limitations. It doesn't mean they have to stop you. Don't be such a selfish bastard. If you have a death wish, that's none of our business, but Maureen's right. All your life, people have had to dance to your tune. Follow your rules. But I'm glad Lora won't. She shouldn't have to. If you love her, you will live for her." He stood. "You'll live for all of us." He turned and left before Justin could see his tears.

Oliver was right. He had to change his ways. Justin knew Lora was the woman he wanted to spend the rest of his life with. And he knew he needed to talk to her parents, especially her father. He was still on medical leave, so he decided to drive over to the

Rices' house. He had called earlier to let them know he wanted to see them.

Mrs. Rice met him at the door with fear or anxiety, Justin wasn't sure which, written all over her face. "Come in. Bernard, um…Mr. Rice is waiting for you." She led Justin into the den. Mr. Rice was sitting in a lounger, and he didn't rise to greet him. He just nodded and pointed to the chair to the side of him.

"So you want to talk to me," he said.

"Yes, I want to let you know I'm serious about your daughter and plan to ask her to marry me if she'll have me…"

Mr. Rice said nothing for a while, but then he turned and looked at Justin.

"You better treat her right. She deserves a man who will be there to support her. Not just as a wife, and mother, but also as a successful scientist."

Justin didn't know what to say. Was this the same bitter man he'd met over Christmas? He was prepared for biting words and a challenge, not caring words from a father who loved his daughter.

"Now, don't think because you're going to be my son-in-law that I'm going to go easy on you," he continued. "I hope you don't plan on coming over here and using all your fancy big words when a short one will do. I don't care what titles you have or awards you've won. I may not have gone to college, but I'm Lora's father and I am who I am, and you'll just have to live with that."

Justin felt like jumping up and shaking his hand but refrained and just nodded his head. "Yes, sir."

Mrs. Rice entered, carrying a tray of hot ginger

tea and biscuits. She glanced in Justin's direction and smiled.

"So when can we expect to have you and Lora over for dinner?"

"Well…"

"You've broken up?" Bernard guessed.

"She's not seeing me right now," Justin said. "But I'm hoping to change that."

"And you need our help?" Grace asked.

He shook his head. "No, I just wanted you to know my intentions."

She nodded, impressed. "Such a gentleman."

"What was the argument about?" Bernard asked.

Justin cleared his throat. He'd hoped to avoid the topic. But he had no choice. "My health."

"You're sick?"

"I was, but I'm not anymore." He sighed. "I have sickle cell anemia."

"Same as that friend of hers?"

"Yes, but I'm going to manage it better."

"That won't do."

"Bernard," Grace scolded.

He held up his hand. "No, don't chastise me. How can a sick man provide for or protect a woman? Would you tie your prize ox to a broken plow?"

"Mr. Rice—"

"I'm sorry, son. It won't do. If that's why Lora won't have you, then she's right." He stood.

Justin stood and blocked his path. "Yes, she had a right to leave me before. But I know what I've lost, and I'm going to get her back whether you want me to or not. I will provide for her and protect her. She will always be cared for. I'm not a broken plow and she's certainly not an ox. We're a man and a woman who are meant to be together."

"So you think."

"I know it."

Bernard sat back down and stared up at the younger man. "You're stronger than I thought," he said with a tone of admiration. "Good luck to you."

"Thank you," Justin said. "You haven't seen the last of me."

"I think I like that boy." Bernard said to Grace as she removed the tray.

"You didn't act like it at first."

"I wanted to see what he was made of. I wanted to see if I could make him leave again."

"But he didn't."

"He knows when to talk and when not to. And he's stubborn. He'll be a good match for my dear Lora."

Grace smiled, relieved that her husband was finally beginning to show his love for his daughter. After sending the letter to Lora, he had spent several days alone in his workshop. She knew not to disturb him. He needed to be alone with his thoughts.

He'd needed to come to terms with his father's treatment of him and his disappointment at never fulfilling his dream. He saw in Lora the same drive and ambition he had had as a child but had never been able to fulfill. Letting go of his resentment and anger hadn't been easy, but it had been a gift.

"He's convinced us," Bernard said. "I hope he'll be able to convince Lora."

* * *

Lora sat in the food court at the mall with Belinda, who had gone on a shopping spree for two friends' upcoming weddings.

"So how are things at work?"

"Fine, but something strange happened."

Belinda leaned forward. "What?"

"Remember that Warren guy I told you about?"

She nodded. "Yes."

"He's disappeared. He just left without a word."

"Good. You won't have to worry about him again."

"I wonder what happened." She paused. "Wait. How do you know I won't have to worry about him?"

"I'm just making a guess." Belinda looked away quickly.

Lora narrowed her eyes. "You know something."

"What could I possibly know?"

"The last I saw him he was leaving Justin's office."

"How is Justin?"

"I heard from Dr. Rollins that he's out of the hospital and is doing well. But don't change the subject."

"Justin's more interesting. When will you see him?"

"It's over."

"Are you sure?"

"I'm not going to love a man with a death wish."

"Men can change." Belinda held up her hands. "Far be it from me to tell you what to do, but if you've got a good man, hang on to him."

"We'll see. Now tell me what you did to Warren."

"Remember that nickname you gave me as a child?"

"Yes."

Belinda smiled, formed her hands into the shape

of a gun and blew on the end of it as if she'd just fired it. "Let's just say that Bullet Belinda accomplished her mission."

Chapter 19

"You know that Lora should be here with you," Maureen said to Justin. He was at the ceremony for Louis to receive a Pet of the Year award to honor his heroic effort to save his master. The ceremony was being held in City Hall and was hosted by the county executive and the local fire department. But Justin didn't seem to care. The most important person to him was missing. He hadn't seen her in two weeks. "Dad and Mom were hoping to see her," Maureen continued.

"They shouldn't have flown in for this," he said. He had tried to convince them that they didn't need to come all that distance for an event that may take only ten or fifteen minutes. But they had been stubborn.

"He saved your life. He's part of the family," his mother said. "Didn't I tell you that you needed him?"

"Yes, and I'll take pictures and send them to you."

"No, I said we are coming and we will. The dog we got for you saves your life, and you don't want us to be there?"

"You know that's not it."

"I'm so glad I trusted my instinct to get you that dog. I can't wait to see him. We've already bought our tickets and packed out bags, and your sister is expecting us."

Justin looked at them now as they sat two seats away. His dad had worn his best suit to the event, and his mother had used the opportunity to buy herself a brand new outfit.

She looked dignified in her dress, matching coat and white gloves. She had grown up in the South, and whenever she went to any kind of formal event, she had to have her purse and white gloves. She said a woman wasn't fully dressed unless she was wearing gloves.

Fortunately, they hadn't mentioned Lora, but he knew if Maureen had her way they would start asking questions. He'd begged his sisters not to mention his breakup with Lora. His medical crisis had upset them enough, and he didn't want them to worry about his relationship, too. His sisters had honored his wishes, but he wasn't sure how long that would last. "Mom and Dad will see Lora another time." Justin sighed, wishing he could get through the ceremony without another mention of her.

"When?" Maureen pressed.

"Soon."

"How soon?"

"Can we just enjoy this moment for now?" he asked, even though he was eager for the event to end. Although all three of his sisters, Ann's husband and her two children were there, along with Oliver and Anya and his parents, he felt empty. Like a part of him was missing. He'd always thought they'd be enough for him. Now he knew he'd been wrong. Lora's absence from his life seemed to grow more evident every day.

He'd missed her the most as he'd prepared Louis for the event. The weekend before he'd found the new dog collar Lora had bought for him. After taking Louis to the groomer for a special bath and to get his nails trimmed, he had the new collar placed on him. Louis wore it now and had been patiently sitting beside Justin but was slowly falling off to sleep.

He knew he'd been stalling. He hadn't yet figured out how best to contact her. What he should say. How he could convince her that he wouldn't be careless with his health again. Justin watched the ceremony, feeling disconnected from everything around him.

Finally, Louis's name was called and Justin stood with him and walked across the stage to get a gold plaque. Louis was not the only animal being honored, and the event lasted two long hours.

At the end of the awards, his parents came over to him and gave him a hug. "We'd expected to see Lora," his mother said.

Maureen folded her arms. "She—"

"Couldn't make it," Justin interrupted.

"Such a shame," Sarah said joining the group. "I'd hoped to see her, too."

Justin sent her a look, but she merely smiled.

"Since we're staying a few days," his mother said. "I hope we get to see her before we go."

Maureen wrapped a hand around Justin's arm. "I'll make sure that he tells her."

"I'm sure you will," Sarah said, then led their parents away to drive them to Ann's house to celebrate.

"Now you're in your element," Maureen said.

"No, I'm not." Justin glanced down at the plaque in his hand. "You know I'm not big into ceremony."

Maureen rolled her eyes. "I'm not talking about the ceremony. I'm talking about your challenge."

"Challenge?"

"Yes." She stood in front of him and rested her hands on her hips like a sergeant issuing orders to a private. "You have a deadline, little brother. Our parents are leaving in four days." She poked his chest with her finger and lowered her voice. "Get Lora back or deal with me."

Carla went to the front desk of the lab, surprised that she had a visitor. She stepped out of the elevators but halted when she saw a man in a suit turn to her. Griffin. He looked like a stranger.

"What are you doing here?"

"I thought it was time I saw where you worked."

"Why?"

"It's important to me."

"Is there a problem, Dr. Patten?" the guard asked.

"No, it's okay." She turned and walked back to the elevators. "I thought we'd agreed to give each other space."

"I did give you space."

Once the elevator doors closed, Griffin drew her to him and kissed her.

Carla tried to push him away, although her body craved more. "What are you doing?"

"You know exactly what I'm doing," he whispered, then kissed her again.

She turned her face away. "I don't want this."

He loosened his grip. "You know, for a while you had me convinced that breaking up was the right thing to do. But then I realized that you need me." When the elevator arrived on her floor, she marched to her office, let him in, then closed the door.

"I need you?" she said, stunned.

Griffin slowly walked around her office with his hands behind his back. "Yes."

"No, I don't."

He turned to her with a smug grin. "Yes, you do. You need me to remind you there's more to life than work." He lifted her up and placed her on the desk, then rested his arms on each side of her. "To make you laugh when you start taking things too seriously. And someone to love you no matter what. I've always been responsible. Now I want to tell you the rest of my story.

"I fell for a woman—Ariel's mother—my parents didn't approve of, and they cut off all ties. I was working on my PhD and then everything changed. We were going to get married, but after Ariel was born she changed her mind and left. Ariel had health issues when she was only two months old. She suffered from RSV."

"RSV?"

"Respiratory syncytial virus," he said. "It's common in infants, but it caused a lot of stress. Our relationship didn't survive. She didn't want, or wasn't ready for, the responsibility of being a mother, so I kept Ariel. Thank God she's fully recovered."

"You have a lot on your plate—"

He straightened and sighed. "I know, and it's too much right now. When I missed your party because of my goal to finish my degree, I realized that I no longer cared about it. I knew I had to make a change. I'm not going to live trying to prove to my parents that I'm not a screwup. I like the work I'm doing, and I can support us. I don't care what anyone says or thinks about our relationship. You need me, and I need you. Not to help me raise my daughter but to just believe in me. You never treat me like a failure. I've put my degree on pause for now. Not for you, but for me. You forced me to see what my priorities are. What I want them to be. All that matters to me is you and Ariel. If you need me to be there for you when you start your new research program, I will. Seeing you happy makes me happy. I can finish my PhD another time if I want to, but this is what I need now. I love you."

"You'd give all that up for me?"

"I don't think I'm giving up anything."

Carla wrapped her arms around his neck and kissed him. She would have kept kissing him if she hadn't heard someone pass by, reminding her that she was still at work. She quickly pulled away. "How serious are you about this?"

"Very."

"What do you think about us moving in together?"

"My place is too small."

"I was talking about my place. My town house is bigger than I need. Think of waking up each morning in a warm bed with me."

"I love the image, but having me move in with you also means having a baby around 24/7."

"I've thought of that."

"Just now?"

"I have a quick mind. I could turn my extra bedroom into Ariel's room and redecorate it in pink, and I want to hand stencil colorful animals on the walls. I can also install an intercom system, you know like those baby monitors, and a closed-circuit TV, so that we see what's going on with her when she's in her room."

"But…"

"Because you are a rather tall man, I'll put my bed in the third bedroom, so we can get a king-size bed for the master bedroom. And don't worry about where your work stuff will go—I have another room that can function as your office. My unfinished basement will be perfect for storing some of your things, and what doesn't fit, we can put in a small storage. It shouldn't cost too much."

He hesitated.

"What is it?"

"I don't want to live off of you. You're giving me so much and—"

"You were right. I need you." She kissed his nose. "And you need me."

"I won't argue with that," he said as his lips descended on hers. They both didn't hear the knock on the door until Lora opened it and peeked her head inside. "Carla?"

They quickly drew apart.

Carla straightened her collar with trembling hands. "Yes?"

Lora looked at them, unable to stop a smile. "I'm just being nosy. Is this *him?*"

Carla couldn't help beaming as she took Griffin's hand. "Yes, it is."

Lora returned to her desk with a smile. Griffin seemed like a nice guy, and she was happy for her friend. At least someone's love life was working out. After falling for a jerk like Warren and then getting her heart broken by Justin, she was ready to stay single for a while.

She was looking at the upcoming lab schedule when the phone rang. She absently picked it up. "Dr. Rice."

"I'd like to talk to you," a deep, familiar voice said, sending a shiver of pleasure and pain through her. She'd been able to guard herself against the sight of him but not his voice. She adjusted her glasses with trembling fingers.

"Can it wait, Dr. Silver?"

"No." He sighed. "I miss you."

Lora took a deep, steadying breath, wishing she could calm her racing heart. Wishing she didn't feel the desire to run into his arms and tell him how much she missed him, too. "Please don't do this to me here."

"You won't answer my calls at home."

He was right. She hadn't spoken to him in weeks. He'd returned to work more than a week ago and they'd held a welcome-back party, but she'd decided not to attend. Since then she'd barely seen him, let alone spoken to him. And all the calls to her home and cell phone had been left unanswered. Now she had to face him. "Okay. I'll be right there." She hung up and then walked to his office.

She would be calm. She wouldn't react to him as she had before. She walked into his office, surprised by how it was the same yet different. Now she knew that the sculpture on his table had been created by Monique. That the Ravens cap had a matching shirt and jacket at home. That he kept a large thermos on his desk to keep from getting dehydrated. She still saw him as a warrior. But this time he wasn't sitting behind his desk—he was standing in front of it, waiting for her. He looked healthy and vibrant, effectively erasing the image of him in the hospital.

She sat and crossed her legs. "Yes, Dr. Silver?"

"Lora—"

"I heard that Louis got an award. Congratulations."

"Thanks. Now Lora—"

"Your family must be so proud."

"They are, but—"

"And if I were you, I'd give Louis his favorite biscuits every day for a year."

"Lora!"

She blinked, feigning innocence. "Yes, Dr. Silver?"

"Stop calling me that."

She clasped her hands in her lap. "What would you like me to call you?"

"I'll get to that. But I wanted you to be the first to know that I'm resigning."

Lora jumped to her feet. "What? Why? When?"

A grin of satisfaction touched the corner of his mouth. "Does the thought of me leaving bother you?"

Lora gathered her emotions, knowing she'd revealed more than she'd wanted to. "You're good at what you do, and you love this job."

Justin lowered his gaze, his lashes shadowing his cheeks. "You once told me I was accomplished as a scientist but a failure as a man."

"That was a long time ago."

He folded his arms, his eyes still lowered. "Not if you still believe that," he said softly.

"You know that I don't."

He lifted his gaze and met hers across the room. "No, I don't. Who do you want to stay?" He pushed himself from the desk and slowly closed the distance between them. "Dr. Silver the scientist, or Dr. Silver the man?" He stopped in front of her, his eyes never wavering. "Which one would you miss more?"

Lora shook her head. She didn't quite know how she felt. She wanted to run, and she wanted to stay. She wanted to scream at him for scaring her and hug him for being all right. "I don't know."

"Yes, you do." He grabbed her shoulders. "You were right, Lora. I don't blame you for leaving. I don't blame you for being unsure right now. Lying in that hospital bed forced me to recognize a lot about myself. I can be selfish and stubborn and arrogant. I like people to do what I tell them and leave me alone. But I also realized something else."

"What?" Lora whispered.

"That I want to be the man in your life. A man you're proud of." He reached inside his pocket and pulled out the good luck stone she'd given him. "I want you to have it."

"You're giving it back?"

"I want you to hold it for me. A warrior needs someone to come home to. When I'm battle worn and weary, I want to come home to you. I have a great family, and I always thought that my work and them would be enough, but these past several weeks without you showed me how wrong I was."

"You'll really take care of yourself from now on?"

"Yes. I promise I'll get regular doctor visits, not overexert, take my supplements and—"

"Listen to me if I'm concerned?"

"Yes, I want to share my life with you. And I—"

Lora placed a finger over his lips. "Are you asking me a question?"

He narrowed his eyes and removed her hand. "You're jumping to conclusions again."

"Am I wrong? You don't want to ask me a special question…?"

He held her hand and kissed the tips of her fingers. "I'm getting to it."

"Get to it faster."

Justin grinned, draping his arms on her shoulders. "Only if the answer is yes."

Lora shook her head, unable to stop a smile of her own. "You have to ask it first."

"Let's try an experiment instead."

"An experiment?"

"Yes. Let's plan a wedding and see who shows up."

She shook her head again. "No, now stop stalling and ask me."

"Okay." Justin took a deep breath, and his eyes darkened with emotion. "Will you marr—"

"Yes."

He laughed. "You didn't let me finish the question."

Lora wiggled her brows. "What matters more, the question or the answer?"

"Neither." He drew her close and held her as if she were the most precious thing to him. "I don't care about being right or wrong, getting accolades or applause. All that matters to me is you."

Lora sunk into the pleasure of his strong embrace. She felt an indescribable happiness, but this time the feeling didn't frighten her. She welcomed it and the years they'd have together.

"I was thinking of a holiday wedding," Justin said.

Lora drew away and stared up at him. "But that's only five months away."

"Then we'd better get started. It's my favorite time of year."

When Lora told her sister she was getting married she was beside herself with excitement. Although Belinda had been married before and the marriage hadn't lasted, she loved weddings. What she liked most was planning weddings, so she took charge but worked closely with Justin's sisters. Maureen took care of the cake and hiring the catering company. Sarah volunteered to find a great DJ for the reception. Ann was recruited to help make hotel arrangements for out-of-town guests, and Belinda was left the main part of choosing the location, ordering the invitations, selecting the colors for the wedding and going shopping with Lora for her wedding dress.

"I know this may sound funny," she said, helping Lora pick her dress, "and I know I've been a bride, but I've always wanted to be a bridesmaid. Now, thanks to you, I get to be one." Their mother had come along with them because she wanted to be there when Lora selected her gown.

After two hours and visiting three bridal stores, Lora finally decided on a waisted wedding gown with a high lace collar and beaded bodice. Belinda couldn't make up her mind what the bridesmaids should wear. However, after consulting with Carla and Sarah, who also were going to be bridesmaids, all three decided on a stylish two-piece white satin outfit. And of course, Monique and Jayla were the flower girls. They and Ariel, although she was not part of the wedding party, would wear a matching dress with a decorative flower headband and tiny gold earrings.

A light snow fell the day of Justin and Lora's wedding. They held the ceremony in a grand hall decorated both for the wedding and the holiday season. Once they were husband and wife, they moved to a reception hall and everyone started to party.

"So, I finally get to dance at your wedding," Oliver said to Justin as the two men stood to the side drinking champagne.

"Yes. I never thought this day would come," Justin replied.

"You're a lucky man. You've found yourself the right woman for you."

Anya came up to them. "We found her for you," she said.

Her husband shook his head. "My dear, you can't take all the credit."

"Of course I can. It was our party that brought them together."

Justin kissed her on the cheek. "You're right. I can never thank you enough."

She blushed. "Now, promise me you'll take good care of my Lora."

"You know I will."

"And, let me know immediately when you plan on making me a godmother."

"Oh, Anya. They haven't even gone on their honeymoon yet."

"The best place to start."

Oliver dragged her away as Anya tried to resist.

Lora came up to Justin and stared at them, curious. "What's going on with them? What are they arguing about?"

He looked at his new bride. "Life's possibilities."

Epilogue

Two years later

> *"Tired of sitting home alone on a Friday night?
> Do you sometimes wonder if Mr. Right will ever
> come? If you have, I've got the answer for you."*

Lora sat on the couch and watched the TV infomercial with a smile of remembrance. Outside a soft snow fell on the new house she and Justin had moved into at the beginning of the year. A seven-foot tree stood in the corner, decorated with lights and ornaments and crowded with presents underneath. Garlands hung on the fireplace and around the railings. She now loved the holidays. She loved shopping for presents and spending time with friends and family. Last week they'd visited Carla and Griffin for dinner, and in a week they'd host both their families. There was still some contention between her father and Justin, but slowly the two men were starting to understand each other. Whenever they discussed current news, her father was relentless in his arguments, and Justin soon began to realize it was easier on everyone if he let him win, or avoided the discussion altogether.

"What are you watching?" Justin asked, taking a seat next to Lora.

"The ghost of Christmas past," she said.

He frowned, staring at the grinning woman on the screen holding up *30 Days to Romance*. "You mean you actually fell for something like that?" Justin asked, looking at her.

Lora nudged him with her elbow, then held up his hand to show him his wedding band. "Hey, don't knock what you don't know. She helped me get you." Lora decided not to tell him that she still had the book, safely stored in the attic with other mementoes.

Justin lowered his head to her stomach and spoke to the baby boy who was due in March. "Your mother still doesn't know."

"Know what?"

His gaze caught and held hers. "You didn't need that book. The moment I set eyes on you, I was yours." His mouth captured hers with the same power with which he'd captured her heart, reminding Lora of all the reasons why she loved the holidays. It was a time of hope, joy, generosity and, above all, love.

* * * * *

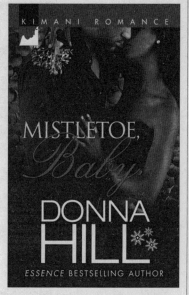